# THE RELEASER

# THE RELEASER

## The Reconciliation Trilogy

## John Elgan

2022
Trumbull, Connecticut

This is a work of fiction. All of the characters, organizations, and events portrayed in this novella are either products of the author's imagination or are used fictitiously.

THE RELEASER

www.johnelgan.com

Library of Congress Control Number: 2022912373

ISBN 978-1-7342430-5-5 (paperback)
ISBN 978-1-7342430-4-8 (ebook)

First Edition: July 2022

*For Joseph and Lori*

# One

*JOINING US LIVE from Florida's space coast and launch
complex 41 at Cape Canaveral as the countdown sequence
begins . . . three victims are dead and at least seven people
injured in shootings overnight, including a woman who . . .
Joshua 10 mission will be Bernie Iverson's record-breaking
thirteenth flight into space . . . sixty-year-old woman died and
a man was in critical condition Saturday following an early
morning . . . has everything you need to succeed, just click . . .
began serving prison time for his second-degree murder
conviction Friday, but officials . . . was charged in court
today with murder and domestic battery in the death of . . .
first with a human aboard and ahead of the largest solar
particle event since the Carrington . . . Why did you feel the
need to kill my son? . . . which claimed the life of a . . . ninety-
days in captivity, she crawled . . . five, four, three, two . . .*

THE SCREEN ZAPPED TO BLACK as the young nurse stretched to
reach the television mounted high on the wall.

Across the room, her patient lay in the hospital bed ogling
her backside. Pulsing veins in his neck plucked a spiderweb
tattoo. "Sorry," the patient grinned and exhaled through rotten
teeth, "Thought I'd lost it again." One of his hands fondled
the television remote beneath the bedsheet, the other twisted
and strained against the cuff to the bed rail.

The nurse closed the room's only window against the
damp chill of the night but made a point to leave a narrow
crack. The patient's breath had so fouled the air in the room

that even the normally stoic policeman who sat beside the window offered a grateful nod.

The nurse crossed the room to adjust the privacy curtain and turned off the lights above the bed. "I go back tomorrow," the patient whispered, running a sweaty hand up her thigh. "How 'bout a bath?"

The nurse recoiled in disgust and embarrassment. He lunged at her.

*Bang!* The policeman's baton struck and scraped along the bed rail. "Ma'am?" he called after the nurse as she rushed out of the room. "Are you all right?" Then turning to the sleazebag, he jabbed him in the chest with the baton and pinned him back in bed. The policeman would deal with him later, first he had to catch up with the nurse.

"Pig! Slut!" the patient cursed and wriggled down beneath the sheets. Within seconds, he let out a thick, mucusy snore. Sleep comes easily for those without a conscience.

Outside the room, lightning flashed. A breeze slipped in through the crack in the window and rippled along the privacy curtain. A dark figure appeared beside the bed.

The patient woke — paralyzed and in terror — suffocated beneath gruesome hands.

*Sscreeeee!* The electric saw made short work of the cranial cap, and latex-gloved hands tugged an organ from a corpse. Beneath bright lights that belied the chill of refrigerated air, two young medical technicians assisted two pathologists in the large, well-equipped basement morgue of New York City's Memorial Hospital.

"Sue," Tom gestured to one of the techs, "more solution here." And feeling the weight of the enlarged spleen in his hand, the pathologist guessed, "Four-twenty-one." He handed the pulpy mass to Sue.

"Three-twenty-five," said Sue, placing the organ in a tray and wiping her hands on her lab coat. "It's our reputation too. Patients dying for no good reason."

"Is there ever a good reason?" said Tom.

"I can think of a few," snickered Kevin, the other tech. And with a look at the spleen, "Four-twenty-five."

"Come on. You guys know what I mean," said Sue. "Jack? You're the boss. What do you think?"

Kevin turned to Jack and knocked the tray beside him, launching the spleen and bloodied scalpels off the table. A hand caught the organ; another hand snagged the scalpels out of the air before they could hit the floor.

"No progress in the city's investigation," replied Jack with the spleen in the palm of one hand and two scalpels bristling from between the fingers of the other. Dr. Jack Wryder, younger but senior of the two day-shift pathologists, looked sharper in his medical whites than most men would in a bespoke suit. Jack handed the spleen to Sue. "Four-fifty-one . . . *point five.*"

Sue was more than a little impressed with Jack's impossible save, and her fawning expression showed it. "But Jack, none of them were expected to die. What about those weird EKG tracings, and —"

"Lunch time," Kevin cut in to break Jack's spell over Sue.

"Let's wrap this guy up and catch some daylight."

Sue batted her eyes at Jack. "Join us today?"

"Thanks, Sue, just a few more things. Don't let me keep you guys."

"All work, no play. I'm not giving up on you, Jack." Sue placed the spleen on a digital scale. Four-fifty-one . . . *point five.*

Jack strolled the hospital corridors. At first glance, he appeared the cool, self-assured physician. A less distracted person, like the child holding her father's hand as he processed a cancer diagnosis, might have noticed something else about Jack. With each step, his spine remained centered over his hips. His body flexed — a coiled spring but without tension — ready for action. His eyes divulged a subtle vigilance. He spied every object, person, entrance, and exit point along the corridor. Jack *was* seeking something, but he did not expect to find it where he was now.

"Hi, Jack," Tracy popped in front of him. She smiled and presented a young woman in scrubs beside her. "I want you to meet Tina." Jack looked confused.

"My friend from London," said Tracy. "Remember? She'll be starting nights."

"Sure . . . yeah." Jack fumbled through his pockets and offered the nurses a mint. Tracy was a notorious close talker.

"Will we work together?" asked Tina, brushing Jack's hand as she took a mint.

"No." Jack replied. "I work —"

"Down in the morgue," Tracy whispered in Jack's face and then raised her voice, "But if you work days, you'll run into Jack visiting patients during lunch. Not his job, just because he's a nice —"

"Nice to meet you, Tina," said Jack. "I'll see you around." And with a modest nod, "Bye, Tracy."

"Bye, Jack," they replied. Tina checked out Jack as he retreated down the corridor. "He's kinda cute . . . in a yummy vicar sort of way. Is he married?"

"Single," Tracy shook her head, "but, like, totally unavailable. Come on. Let's meet the interns."

---

Jack crept into a patient's room. Children's books and toys littered the bed. Beside the bed, kneeling on the cold, hard floor, prayed a little girl, Emily Shire. The top of Emily's tiny head was barely visible from where Jack stood silently inside the doorway. He saw an inconspicuous spot of light above her head. She sensed Jack's presence.

"Jack!" Emily screeched and leapt onto the bed.

"Hey squirt."

"Look at my hair." Emily turned her head to reveal a long braid. "Tracy did it."

"Wow," said Jack.

Emily's scrunched up face showed that Jack's response fell short of what she needed to hear. "Do you like it?" she pressed.

"You look beautiful," replied Jack. "Maybe I should get one." Jack picked up a Slinky from the bed and dangled the spring from the top of his head.

"Nooo," giggled Emily.

A shrill voice intruded from outside in the hallway, "Nice hat . . . *Sauriel.*" The voice belonged to hospital orderly, Raul Noma. He lurked in the hall outside Emily's room.

Emily scowled and looked at Jack. "Your name isn't Sreal."

Jack pointed to the middle initial printed on his hospital ID tag: Dr. Jack S. Wryder. "My middle name. It's pronounced *Sauriel.*"

"William Francis Cole. Hey, *Francis!*" screeched Raul. He was reading personal information from patient charts he had pilfered from the nurses' station.

"Eejit!" A burly nurse snatched the charts out of Raul's long, unclipped fingers. "I'm sure ya got your own work to do, so go on and do it."

Emily took Jack's hand and pulled him close. "I don't like him," she whispered in his ear while keeping an eye on Raul through the doorway. "He scares me." A greasy raven in scrubs, Raul strutted about the nurses' station.

Jack observed Raul's face. To Jack, Raul's eyes, nostrils, lips, and ears appeared reddened and flu-like. "Some people just tease," Jack assured Emily, and he proceeded to tickle her into a giggling frenzy and playful screeches.

"Okay Emily." A pediatric nurse entered the room with a wheelchair. "Circus is over. Time for therapy."

Emily used her most doe-eyed look on Jack. "Come visit me again?"

"Okay, squirt, I'll do my best to sneak back."

Emily poked a pinky at Jack. "Promise me you'll come

back?"

"Promise," Jack hooked Emily's pinky in his, "I'll be back."

Emily called after Jack as he disappeared from the room. "I like stuffed animals!"

Jack smiled.

Jack entered the elevator. The door closed, and the inverted red triangle glowed — going down. He exited onto a quiet floor and made his way directly to the room of Mrs. Lopez.

Ravaged by a terminal illness, Mrs. Lopez lay in bed and stared at the ceiling. A nurse reached beneath the foot of the bed. "Mrs. Lopez, I'm going to adjust your bed slightly." She traded whispers with Jack.

"Hi, Jack."

"How is she?"

"Hours at most."

"Where's the family? They'd been here all week."

"On their way."

The nurse excused herself, and Jack stood at the foot of the bed alone with Mrs. Lopez. He saw an inconspicuous spot of light above her head.

Mrs. Lopez sensed Jack's presence. Her eyes grew wide, and she raised a frail, trembling hand and pointed at Jack.

"Santa Muerte. Santa Muerte!" she groaned then fainted as the nurse returned to the room with the Lopez family. Jack slipped out of the room.

As Jack breezed down the corridor, Tina spied him through an open doorway. She pulled her scrub top tight and poked her head out of the supply closet. "Dr. Jack. Dr. Jack, can you help me?"

"Sure, Tina." Jack walked back, and she withdrew into the closet.

Tina pointed to a stack of linens high atop a shelf. Jack noticed a step stool she could have used, but he decided to step inside and reach for the linens. Tina kicked out the door stop and sidled up behind Jack. The door snapped shut.

"Any more mints?" Tina purred and plunged both hands into Jack's pant pockets.

Jack jumped, tripped over the step stool, and escaped out of the room.

As Tina sat alone and dejected upon the stool, the door reopened — just wide enough for Jack to toss a roll of mints inside.

As Jack made his getaway from what was turning out to be an afternoon of awkward events, a painful groan drew his attention. The sound had come from the room of Ben Fuller, an elderly patient that he knew well. Jack had planned on visiting Ben earlier. That was before Mrs. Lopez called him out and Tina had launched her surprise attack. Pausing in the doorway, Jack saw an inconspicuous spot of light above Ben's head. He watched two nurses tend to Ben.

"He's in God's hands now," said one nurse. "I wish we could do more."

"He could go on like this for months," said the other.

"Tough ol' bastard. Aren't you, Ben? No fear. 'To be absent from the body is to be present with the Lord.'"

"Well, if there is a God, I can't imagine how He can let him endure this. It's torture, really."

Jack brooded over Ben's suffering as he waited for an elevator. What was the point of so much pain? And besides, we're wasting time. The doctors and nurses may be unable to help, but Jack reasoned he could do something.

The elevator door opened. "Are you going down?" asked a passenger.

"Yeah," Jack replied, "all the way."

---

"You missed another good one," Kevin chided Jack.

*Another* good one? Jack wondered.

Kevin added, "New place 'round the corner makes one helluva margarita."

Jack's attention waned. *Of course, Kevin doesn't know.*

"Maybe too guh . . . ood," Sue hiccupped. "Lucky they're already dead before you touch'em, Kev."

Tom appeared to be the sober one. "Jack, you really ought to come out with us sometime. You have to eat, right? Take a real break and get some fresh air. You're going to go nuts driving yourself so hard down here."

"Thanks, Tom. One of these days."

"One of these *days*?" said Sue, giving Jack a light shoulder bump. "You've been here six months and you —"

Kevin placed himself between Jack and Sue. "So, Jack, how's everything up in the land of the livin'? Any new business comin' our way?"

"Kevin, you are pathetic," said Sue. "Please, it would be

great to have just one day with no deaths. Restore my faith in meh . . . medicine."

"Then we'd be outta work," quipped Kevin. "Speakin' of medical screw-ups. Have you heard the story 'bout the guy who was admitted for an appendectomy but instead they cut off —"

"Here we go," said Sue. "I don't know how your wife puts up with you seven days a week."

The doors crashed open, and an orderly rolled in a body. Tom lifted the sheet. It was Mrs. Lopez. Jack examined the corpse and fixated on an inconspicuous spot of light he saw above her head. Tom followed Jack's gaze. "What's up, Jack?"

"What?" Jack turned to Tom. "Nothing. It's late. We'll put Mrs. Lopez in the queue for tomorrow."

Jack remained in his scrubs while his colleagues had logged out for the day and changed into their civvies.

"Kevin," said Tom, "could you complete the papers on Lopez? I promised my daughter I'd be at her soccer game."

"I dunno, Tom. My wife will get awfully angry if I'm late again."

"Well, if it's going to be that much trouble for you to —"

"I'll take care of it, Tom," said Sue, reaching for the patient file in Tom's hands. "I'll make a note on the tests. Go to your daughter's game."

Kevin glared at Sue. "You're not certified for that kinda work. You start it. I'll finish it up," he said, and then to Tom,

"You owe me another one, big guy."

"Thank you, *Sue*," said Tom, handing her the file on his way out. "I really appreciate it."

Sue took a swipe at Jack with the file. "So, you have any exciting plans for tonight?"

"Maybe take in a movie."

"Wow," Kevin mocked Jack. "A movie? You gotta live it up a little. One day you'll be scramblin' outta here to your kid's basketball game."

"*Soccer* game, you jerk. And why do you have to hassle Tom like that?"

Kevin snatched the file from Sue. "Easy there, big guns. Let's just fill out the forms on our way out and drop'em off together." He grinned back at Jack. "Don't do anythin' I would do. The excitement might kill ya." Aside to Sue, "After we leave, he probably invites the nurses down and —" Sue elbowed Kevin, who winced, "Maybe we should work late."

Jack glimpsed Sue's hand reach for Kevin's as they left the morgue, and the door closed behind them. Their footsteps faded down the hall.

Jack locked and leaned back against the door. His head ached, and he rubbed his temples. He removed a small, unlabeled bottle from his pocket, shook a few pills into his hand and swallowed them. He closed his eyes.

The toe tag read "Lopez, Maria Rosa." Jack peeled back the sheet covering her face. He cupped one hand and held it motionless, palm down, above her forehead. He waited. Across Jack's skin from fingertips to elbow, dark stripes began to appear, and one by one, like passing clouds, the rippling bands traveled across his skin and disappeared beneath his sleeve.

Mrs. Lopez's face began to glow and brighten. A spot of light emerged from her forehead and took the shape of a gleaming sphere that floated beneath Jack's cupped hand. Jack looked up. Above them, he saw a pinwheel of spiraling stars and whirling light. At its core, the spiral emitted a brilliant light. He moved his hand aside and allowed the sphere to float up and disappear into the light, which winked out with a flash.

Satisfied he no longer saw a spot of light above Mrs. Lopez's head, he pulled the sheet over the corpse.

Jack hesitated outside the drawer of another body that had been brought in that day; a serial rapist who had died unexpectedly before he was scheduled to return to prison. He opened the drawer, slid out the tray and peeled back the sheet. Above a spiderweb tattoo on his neck, Jack saw the man's eyes, nostrils, lips, and ears as reddened and flu-like. "You shouldn't be here," Jack admonished the corpse. "Not yet. Not today."

This time, Jack cupped *both* of his hands above the corpse's forehead. Dark stripes appeared on Jack's skin and shimmered up his arms.

The redness in the man's face intensified, concentrated in the forehead, and thickened into a sooty, blood-red coagulation that emerged from his head as a throbbing, tumor-like mass. The mass hovered beneath Jack's cupped hands.

Jack saw stars form and swirl above him. But rather than move his hands aside, Jack confined the throbbing mass, jerking and twitching beneath his hands, and directed it away from the spiraling galaxy. He pushed the revolting object toward the floor.

As the trembling mass began to rise toward the light, a twisted, clawed hand erupted from out of the floor and snatched it below.

# Two

THE NEON SIGN BUZZED, "All Are Welcome." Beneath the sign, a few homeless people milled about in the light of an open doorway on an otherwise dark and empty street. Across the street, a lamp cast long, misty shadows on damp pavement. Out of the shadows, a dark figure emerged. In its clutch, a torn-out headline read "Heiress to Nurse, Sarah Ward Opens Homeless Shelter."

Inside the shelter, in the corner of a small, gray-walled room, a young woman and her four-year old child shrank upon gray metal chairs beside a gray metal desk. Eyes cast down, the young woman whimpered an apology. "We didn't know where to go."

Sarah softly rose from her chair behind the desk and knelt beside the young woman. She placed a tender hand on the woman's cheek and combed aside her tousled hair. "You are not alone," whispered Sarah. There was an obliging clarity in Sarah's eyes, and deeper yet, a soulful tug from Sarah's own pain, which she had suffered for far more years than her smooth skin revealed.

The young woman sobbed, her shoulders dropped, and all the tension in her body melted away. Through bruised and swollen eyes, she surrendered a little smile to the warmth of Sarah's gaze and gathered her child closer in a hope-filled hug.

The child's attention was fixed on the wide grin and fiery mohair of a vintage Troll Doll — the sole keepsake in Sarah's otherwise austere office.

"You can keep it." Sarah trotted the doll off the edge of her desk and handed it to the child, who began to stroke the doll's hair in the same way Sarah had comforted her mother.

Sarah gently grasped the young woman's hands and lifted her to her feet. "I'll help you get comfortable here. Gideon will go to your apartment and gather your things."

"But it's not safe there. He —"

"Gideon will take care of it," Sarah assured her, and turning to Gideon, whose super-heavyweight physique filled the doorway, "Won't you, Gideon?"

———

Sarah appeared, angelic, in the light of the shelter doorway. Across the street, the dark figure stirred in the shadows. Sarah stepped off into the night.

It followed her.

"Ms. Ward," a voice cried out, "Ms. Ward!" Sarah turned, and the dark figure withdrew.

A man in a long, tattered, black overcoat and greasy baseball cap grasped Sarah's hands. He stared into her eyes. "Thank you. God bless you, ma'am. I'll remember you. God bless you. God bless you, ma'am."

Sarah nodded with a smile, and with a glance at the shadows behind the man, she proceeded alone.

The dark figure stalked Sarah, lithely moving from shadow to shadow, its footsteps lost among the sounds of the city: hush of distant tires on damp pavement, rumble of panel trucks making late night deliveries, and the low growl of the subway beneath their feet. Sarah turned a corner.

The dark figure charged across the street, closed the distance, and rounded the corner.

"Can I help you?" Sarah stood defiant in the middle of the sidewalk.

The dark figure was very tall and wore a heavy, black oilskin drover which, along with his hair, was slicked with a full night's rain. His face was obscured in darkness.

"Help me? No. No, thank you," he replied evenly but not entirely without surprise. His legs concealed by the mist, Jack Wryder appeared to float as he retreated back around the corner.

"Give me your phone," the slimy hustler demanded with a squirrely scan down the deserted alley. The young waif gave up her phone, and the hustler pressed the handle of a knife into her sweating palm. He figured it was about time to profit from the months of grooming it took to gain her trust: vicious cycles of reward and punishment and isolating her from anyone who cared about her. "Now, this time," he gritted his teeth up close to her face, "get it right."

The young waif cast her eyes down past her worn clothes to the dark pavement beneath her feet. He pushed up her chin with a dirty knuckle. "Hey, look at me," he shouted. "I took you in. I protect you." And he softened his tone, "Show me you really care, huh. Make me proud."

She nodded.

"I can't hear you," he pinched and twisted the skin on her chin.

"Yes," she winced.

Jack climbed the unlit stoop of his apartment building – a modest pre-World War II walk-up, chosen for its convenient location across from the bus and subway stops. The new energy-saving bulb above the entrance had failed again. The original light fixture, like so many other features of the old building seemed to chew up and spit out anything modern. But for Jack, the worst thing about a walk-up apartment was the opportunity to get to know your neighbors, which is why he had bought up most of the building's apartments. The only other tenants, a misanthropic live-in super and an octogenarian couple, occupied the ground floor. It was late, the super would be asleep, and the light outside the entrance would need to be taken care of before the old couple descended the stairs on their early morning bagel run. Jack reached inside the lamp above the entrance to unscrew the bulb but discovered that someone had already removed it.

"I don't want no trouble, mister." The waif's voice shook as much as the knife she held to Jack's spine. "Just gimme your wallet."

Jack slowly turned. An inconspicuous spot of light flickered above the shadowy outline of the trembling teen. Jack brushed aside the knife and moved in close to her.

He gazed deep into her eyes. "'Do not be afraid nor discouraged,'" Jack spoke with calm confidence. "You don't have to do this."

She stepped back and pointed the knife at Jack's face.

"Just gimme your wallet."

Jack saw her eyes and nostrils redden and the light above her head fade. He inched toward her and up to the tip of the knife, which pressed against his throat.

"Return home," he whispered. "They will not be angry with you. They will understand this time."

The waif's eyes welled up with tears, and she coughed. The suffocating grip of all the guilt she felt, all the fear, and the anxiety which had possessed her for so long began to loosen as a bitter phlegm in her chest. She coughed it up and spit it out. All of it. And taking a deep, clear breath, she let the knife slip from her hand. She bound down the steps and across the street.

Jack looked after her as she climbed onto a city bus — above her head, he saw the spot of light return. Right, he thought, back to the task of restoring a different light, and he turned his attention to the entrance lamp.

The hustler scooped up the knife and plunged it into Jack's back, grunting as he repeatedly stabbed into him.

Jack seized the hustler's knife-hand and tightened his grip. With a bone-crushing snap, the knife dropped from the hustler's hand and *rattled* down the steps. Jack grabbed him by the throat with one hand and lifted him off his feet, pinching his fingertips together behind the windpipe. He saw the hustler's eyes, nostrils, lips, and ears as reddened and flu-like.

"They'll have to wait for yours," said Jack, and he tossed the hustler — broken, gasping, but alive — down the steps to the sidewalk.

Inside the building, Jack climbed two flights of stairs and

entered his unlocked, unlit apartment. He easily navigated through the darkness past a couple of thickly upholstered chairs, a floor lamp, and a small potted tree. Jack poked his fingers through the knife holes in the back of his damp coat and let the damaged drover slip to the floor. He reclined deep into the chair closest to the lamp and felt his way up beneath its vintage shade to the smooth, cold bulb; he would use it to replace the missing bulb outside the entrance. But first . . . head aching, he rubbed his temples, removed a small, unlabeled bottle from his pocket, shook a few pills into his hand and swallowed them. Then he closed his eyes.

"Out for a late-night stroll, Sauriel?" a lofty voice inquired in the dark. "Or do you now prefer Jack?"

Jack yanked the lamp chain, and light bounced about the high coffered ceilings brightening the room. A hefty man in his seventies filled the chair across from Jack. He wore the smart, three-piece herringbone tweed of a college professor but the hard visage of a medieval warrior king.

"Gabriel? I wasn't going to . . ."

". . . murder Sarah Ward?" Gabriel enunciated through hair that hung about his face like raw, steel wires. "Which is precisely what it would be Sauriel, murder."

Gabriel gestured toward the lamp, which glowed brightly beside Jack. "You have begun to behave and think more as Jack Wryder. Perhaps you are becoming too close to them." He picked a tiny, brown leaf from the base of the potted tree next to his chair. Upon the brittle leaf was written a name: "Maria Rosa Lopez."

"You release the souls of the human dead," said Gabriel.

And meeting Jack's eyes, "Your mission at the hospital is very specific, Sauriel."

"I can do more than this . . . this menial task. Restore my *full* powers, Gabriel, so I can fight in the battles to control —"

"Control the forces of darkness when you cannot even control yourself?"

"But Gabriel . . ."

"Prove that you are capable of succeeding in *this* assignment, and perhaps in a millennium, you will be granted the role you seek."

"A thousand years? I can't wait that long."

"Your impatience, your problem with authority, and your disregard for the rules, is what landed you in this position, Sauriel. We're beginning to wonder. Are you up to the task?" Gabriel sank back in the chair. "You are not the only one. There are others prepared to take your place."

"But I don't see enough guardians of good to —"

"You do not *see* because it is not your duty to see. The battle is being waged by others."

"Gabriel, something on Earth is shifting the balance toward evil. I can feel it. At the hospital, I *see* it — too many souls are going to the other side. Today, I released the soul of a rapist. But it wasn't supposed to be his time."

"Sauriel —"

"We need more good souls to become guardians. Otherwise . . ." Jack spoke faster and louder, "the humans will be powerless."

"Sauriel, these ideas of yours are reckless and corrupt."

"I have the power —"

"But not the authority, Sauriel!"

Jack persisted, "Well maybe not the healthy ones . . ."

"If your soul was corrupted by the premature death of even a single human, whatever your intention, it would give the forces of darkness the advantage to prevail over the Earth — *your* powerful soul, Sauriel!"

". . . just the sick and suffering," Jack continued, oblivious to Gabriel's admonition.

The apartment shook. Gabriel rose from the chair and six wings of fire leapt from his shoulders. Jack closed his eyes against an inextinguishable light.

Gabriel thundered, "The healthy, the sick, young or old, not a single human soul shall be released before its time."

# Three

FLASHES FROM THE INVESTIGATOR'S CAMERA lent a
celebratory feel to the murder scene. On the floor beside a
sushi bar lay the blood-stained body of a restaurant worker.
Through an opening behind the bar, the kitchen staff gawked
at the body and the odd pair of plainclothes detectives who
questioned the restaurant manager.

Veteran Detective Frank Kelly, a middle-aged Bronx
bulldog, strained the waistband of his crumpled navy blue suit
as he leaned heavily on the counter. Beside him, stood an
attentive young Indian detective, Vijay Vashi. Vijay was yin
to Frank's yang — soccer player build tucked into a pressed
suit, ready smile. Vijay was on secondment from India
through an international exchange program.

"Okay," said Frank towering over the manager. "Let's go
over this part one more time. You're in the front of the
restaurant, over there at the table by the front door, foldin'
napkins. You don't hear, or see, or notice anything at all?"

"I look up when customer begin to scream," replied the
manager.

"And that's when you see this guy," Frank gestured at the
dead man on the floor, "walk out of the kitchen, bleedin', and
collapse on the floor in the middle of your restaurant."

"I look up when customer yell. He already on floor when I
see him."

Frank turned to Vijay with a drowsy roll of his eyes.
"Nobody seen anythin'."

Vijay stepped aside and took a seat by the door. "Frank, if
the manager was sitting here, by the front door, he would

have seen anyone leave the restaurant."

"Mr. Waki," Frank puckered his mouth, "at any time before, or after, you heard your customers scream, did you notice anyone leave the restaurant?"

"No. I sit facing bar. I have unfolded napkins on left side of table and . . ."

*Rattling* metal from the kitchen caught Frank's attention. One of the cooks hopped down from a table. On the kitchen wall above the table, was a large metal vent. Frank whispered to Vijay and signaled a uniformed officer to follow him into the kitchen. Vijay disappeared out the front door.

The cook bolted.

Frank and the officer pursued the cook, crashing their way through the kitchen and out the back door. In the alley behind the restaurant, they found the cook, pinned up against the wall. Vijay held a tight grip on the cook's arm.

Frank, out-of-breath and red in the face, confronted the cook. "Why the hurry little fella?" To which the cook replied with a blank stare.

"Collar 'im," Frank barked to the officer. "Vijay, back inside with me. He stashed something in the wall. And," Frank hesitated but the words managed to escape, "Good job."

Vijay considered Frank's nonathletic build. "Well Frank, I figured you didn't need the exercise."

Inside the kitchen, Frank stacked milk crates and climbed atop the table below the metal vent in the wall. He searched his empty pockets. "Vijay, you cops from India carry flashlights, don't ya?"

Frank shined Vijay's penlight into the vent. Deep inside

the vent, light glinted off the blade of a knife.

"Bingo!" Frank reached for the knife. He stretched into the vent with one hand covered in a plastic evidence bag, the other held the penlight. He grasped at the knife, and it slipped from his plastic-wrapped fingers and slid deeper into the vent. "Shit!" He stretched farther inside the vent and seized the knife. "Gotcha." As Frank backed out of the vent, his belt buckle caught the lip of the opening, and he wriggled to free himself. He was stuck.

Frank sucked in his gut and had another, unsuccessful, go at it. "Son of a . . ." Maybe, he thought, if he could relax his body. Frank focused on the flickering penlight. Calm and composed for another attempt, he exhaled slowly — into the face of the rat that had turned the corner inside the vent. Whiskers bristling in Frank's breath, the rat was as surprised as Frank. Almost.

"Shiii . . . shoo. Shoo!" Frank made stabbing gestures with the knife in his hand. "Back off. Back off or I'll skewer you."

The penlight flickered and faded. Frank banged the light against the wall of the duct.

"Frank? Frank, is everything all right?" Vijay's muffled voice sounded inside the vent.

The rat crawled toward Frank. The penlight winked out.

"Get me outta here. Get me outta here, now!"

Vijay used a heavy butcher's knife to pry the vent cover from the wall, and Frank broke loose out of the duct, crouched atop the table, and completely disheveled. The splintered vent cover hung about Frank's waist like a hula skirt. Cameras flashed, and cheers erupted from the small crowd of officers and crime scene investigators that had gathered in the kitchen.

"What? What?" Frank asked. "Vijay, don't just stand there, gimme a hand, *partner*."

Frank stepped down and gave the evidence bag with the knife to one of the investigators, and the penlight he handed — twisted and broken — to Vijay. Vijay gaped at the penlight and then back at the rubbled hole in the wall.

Outside the restaurant, Vijay took the driver's seat in the unmarked police car, and Frank regarded his disheveled reflection in the side mirror with a frown. "Great. Just great."

Vijay snickered. Frank glared at him.

<hr>

A mouse scurried past Jack and disappeared under the door to the morgue. Jack smiled and locked the door behind him. "Good night, Jerry."

The elevator opened to a quiet hospital lobby, and as Jack stepped out, he saw that Tina had arrived to begin her night shift. She was headed straight toward the elevator. Jack attacked the "Door Close" button. Before the doors closed, five haughty men in scrubs barged into the elevator.

"Surgical pavilion. Eleven," one of the surgeons bellowed at Jack, who was pressed up against the button panel as much by their oversized egos as their clumsy bodies. The nearest of them read Jack's ID.

"Wryder, huh. So, this is the guy my patients gush about."

Jack shrugged and looked away to press eleven. A patronizing hand clasped his shoulder. "Hear the one about the sociable pathologist?" said the surgeon with a smirk to his colleagues. "He stares at *your* shoes when he talks."

The surgeons had a good laugh before the elevator doors opened for Jack — third floor, Oncology. "What's the difference between God and a surgeon?" asked Jack as he swiped across *all* the floor buttons and stepped off. "God knows he's not a surgeon."

"Son of a . . ." The elevator doors closed.

Jack found peace on the quiet ward. The frenetic pace and noises of the day shift staff had given way to the cold hush of empty corridors. It was here, among these cancer patients, that Jack had made a personal connection with this world. It was a place of deep despair, high hopes, and a fixed purpose.

A faint groan beckoned Jack to a patient's room at the far end of the corridor. He passed the unoccupied nurse's station; Tina would have been there by now, but someone had pressed all the elevator buttons. Jack peered inside the patient's room. The medical monitor cast a wispy green hue over a man who lie groaning in pain.

Tina had arrived at the nurses' station moments before a patient alarm *blared* from the monitoring console. In a panic, she tried to interpret the station's digital display. The location of the alarm read "35A Ben Fuller."

Tina raced toward Ben's room and glimpsed the figure of a man turn the corner at the far end of the corridor. She called out, "Jack?"

With one white-knuckled hand, Frank clutched the door, in the other a doughnut shook to pieces with each bump and swerve of the car. Vijay smiled and waved apologies to the other drivers and pedestrians, who returned obscene gestures as he and Frank barreled down the city street.

The radio crackled to life. "NYPD we have a 10-34 at Memorial Hospital."

Frank released his death grip on the door to grab the radio. "Detective Kelly responding to the 10-34 at Memorial."

Vijay turned to Frank. "10-34. An assault in progress at the hospital."

"Yeah, that's right. You got the codes." Frank pointed ahead. "Now, eyes on the road."

Vijay swerved to avoid another collision.

"If you'd learn to drive," said Frank, "we might even get there alive."

"I can't help it if you people drive on the wrong side." Vijay swerved again, narrowly avoiding a collision. This time, he offered an obscene gesture.

"You picked up that skill pretty quick. How much longer are you with us?"

"Eight more months, Frank. A total of nine here in New York. Then to Dulles Airport for three months sponsored by your FBI."

"Let's just hope the Feds don't put you in a cockpit."

"Frank, you should come to India. The exchange program is a great opportunity."

"Great opportunity? No. Over there I couldn't tell you guys apart."

"It's just as well, Frank. Too few doughnut shops in Mumbai."

A street sign for the hospital was visible.

"Okay," said Frank. "Careful, we're almost there. Take the next right, and park after the emergency entrance."

"Frank, is this call typical?"

"Several suspicious deaths over the past seven months. Eyes on road. Turn here."

"Seven months, Frank?"

"Last week, someone noticed that some charts for patients were missin'. That's what got people's attention. Otherwise, nobody would've noticed. People are always dyin' in hospitals. That's why I stay away from hospitals and doctors. Focus on the road."

"Like you said, Frank, sick people die in hospitals. What makes these deaths suspicious?"

"No natural cause of death or sign of physical trauma. No evidence of chemical agents or medical malpractice. Just somethin' with the EKGs that the doctors find —"

*Sirens blared* from behind. Vijay veered out of the way of an ambulance, crossed a lane of oncoming traffic, and stopped with a *bump* to the curb.

Frank escaped out of the car and hopped onto the sidewalk. "The right side of the road! In the United States . . . it's the right side of the road! Just . . . go park the car." Frank left Vijay behind and entered the hospital through a set of automatic doors. As the doors slid closed behind Frank, Vijay pulled out.

Frank flinched at the *crunch* of a low-speed collision but didn't break stride.

A small, chatty group of hospital staff had gathered just outside Ben Fuller's room. Police tape hung loosely across the doorway, and a uniformed cop stood guard. Frank swaggered up to the crowd.

"I'm Detective Kelly. Who made the call?"

The crowd hushed and an older woman in a crisp white uniform stepped forward.

"I made the call, Detective. I'm the head nurse on the night shift. Dana White."

Frank lifted the police tape. "Ms. White, could we move inside? And he and the head nurse stepped inside the doorway. "What happened here?"

"After we failed to resuscitate the patient, we examined the rhythm strip. We saw the suspicious EKG tracings we were told to look for, and I called security. It was around 10 p.m."

"You said, 'we'. Who was with you when you arrived in the room?"

"Well, Tina was already in the room checking the monitor when —"

"You weren't the first to arrive? Tina? Who's Tina?"

"I'm over here," a voice squeaked.

Frank poked his head outside the room. Tina resembled an enthusiastic schoolgirl, hand raised high and waving.

"Tina," said Frank, "come in here please." To the head nurse, "Please wait right outside, while I speak with her."

Tina raised the police line tape which detached from the doorway and clung to her like plastic wrap. Tina shook free of the tape and tripped into the room.

"Hi," said Tina.

"Hi," Frank mimicked. "Can I get your full name, please?

"Tina Martinez. Tina Patricia Martinez. I just started here. I used to work at —"

"Tonight. Tell me what happened here tonight."

"It was, like, really quiet at the station. The nurses' station. You would have walked past it. I was alone and this is my first night here. And, like, all of a sudden, the alarms for Mr. Fuller go off. I buzzed the head nurse on duty. You met her. Dana —"

"White. You alerted the head nurse. Then you . . .?"

"I ran down to Mr. Fuller's room. He didn't respond. He had no pulse, and he wasn't breathing. I was about to try and resuscitate him. Then she and Dr. Marshall came in."

"Before you called, who else was on the floor? Other nurses, hospital staff, patients out of bed?"

Tina shook her head. "It was totally dead." Her eyes widened in embarrassment. "I mean, like, really really quiet."

"I understand. You were alone. After you alerted the head nurse, you . . .?"

"I ran here as fast as I could."

"Did you notice anyone as you left your station and approached this room?"

"I was the only one. No, wait. I did see a man at the very end of the hall. It looked like Jack, but he didn't turn around."

"Jack? Who is Jack?"

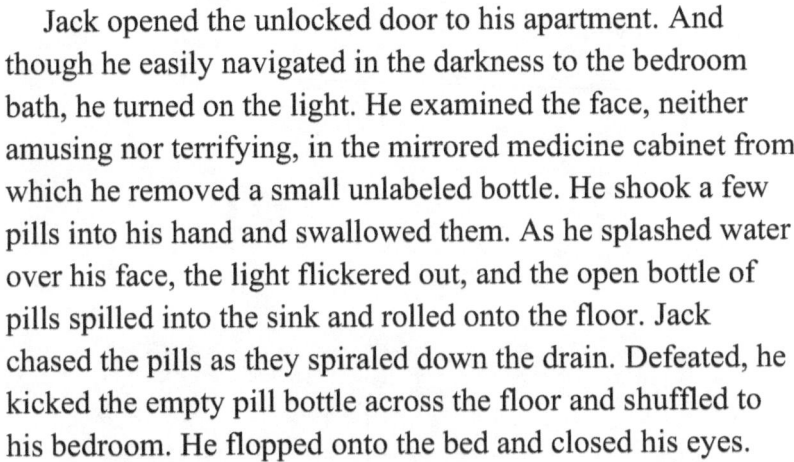

Jack opened the unlocked door to his apartment. And though he easily navigated in the darkness to the bedroom bath, he turned on the light. He examined the face, neither amusing nor terrifying, in the mirrored medicine cabinet from which he removed a small unlabeled bottle. He shook a few pills into his hand and swallowed them. As he splashed water over his face, the light flickered out, and the open bottle of pills spilled into the sink and rolled onto the floor. Jack chased the pills as they spiraled down the drain. Defeated, he kicked the empty pill bottle across the floor and shuffled to his bedroom. He flopped onto the bed and closed his eyes.

The apartment shook with a *thunderclap*. Jack emerged from the bedroom, the thorny scent of roses stung his eyes and nostrils, and he squinted at a torrent of light. The potted tree was ablaze in the living room. And Gabriel appeared in angelic splendor. Two flaming wings were raised above Gabriel's head, the tips of which curled to the high ceiling, and four more were extended at his sides as a wall of fire that spanned the entire width of the apartment.

"Sauriel," Gabriel's voice boomed, "you have committed offense against man and the Almighty. For your offense against the Almighty, you are stripped of all your powers. Now Sauriel, you truly are the human, Jack Wryder."

"For your offense against man, you must save no fewer than one-hundred human souls. This is your repentance. If you fail to save one-hundred souls before the death of your own, now mortal, body — *your* soul will be doomed to serve the forces of darkness. Repent, Jack Wryder. Repent. The balance of power in the heavens and fate of this world now depend upon you."

# Four

"DR. WRYDER. DR. JACK WRYDER! This is Detective Kelly from the New York City Police Department." Pounding on the door woke Jack from a heavy sleep. He rose from bed, and the room spun wild. His vision was distorted. His ears rang. As Jack stumbled toward the door, it swung open wide. Frank and Vijay stood shoulder to shoulder and stared.

Except for the narrow shafts of morning light that slipped in between them, the apartment was pitch black, and all that the detectives could see was Jack — puffy-eyed, sallow, and sweaty.

"Dr. Wryder?" Frank glanced at a photocopy of Jack's hospital ID. "Jack S. Wryder?"

Jack nodded and held his throbbing head.

"Rough night?" asked Frank. "Wanna talk about it?"

"You said . . . you were police," replied Jack. "What is it? Someone in trouble?"

Frank leaned forward to step inside, but Jack waved him off.

"You are a pathologist at Memorial Hospital?" asked Vijay.

Jack nodded.

"We're investigatin' the recent death of a patient at Memorial," said Frank. "The deceased's name is Ben Fuller."

"Ben?"

"Dr. Wryder, you know Ben Fuller?

"Yes. He suffers from bone cancer. Ben is a patient in the oncology ward."

"*Was* a patient." Frank strained to see inside the apartment beyond Jack.

"You were not his doctor," said Vijay. "What was your relationship with Mr. Fuller?"

"Relationship?" Jack mumbled. "I visit Ben . . . when he's not . . . in too much pain."

Frank shot Vijay an 'I got this' look and leaned in to catch Jack's eye. "When was your last visit with Mr. Fuller?"

"Yesterday. But he was in terrible pain."

"What time did you last see Mr. Fuller?"

"It was around the time they serve lunch . . . maybe noon."

"Are you sure the last time you saw Ben Fuller was 'round noon yesterday? Any help we can get to narrow down the time."

"No. I did see Ben later. I stopped by on my way out. It would have been around . . . I don't know."

"Were you alone with Ben last night? 'Round, what time did you say? Ten o'clock?"

"I didn't say. It was late. He was in great pain. I don't recall seeing any of the staff. I may have —" Gabriel's voice resounded in Jack's skull.

"Repent, Jack Wryder. Repent."

Jack sweat hard. Even the yellow pallor had drained from his face.

"Jack, it's important you recall when you were alone with Ben last night. Around ten, was it?"

Jack stared, distant and closed off.

"Jack, can you try and focus on the time you were with Ben Fuller? It was around ten and you were in Mr. Fuller's

34

room, Ben's room. You saw Ben lyin' on his bed. Ben was alive but in pain. Then what happened, Jack?"

"I'm sorry. I can't. My head feels . . ." Jack could not support the weight of his head which hung about his shoulders, eyes cast down to his pill bottle, which lay open and empty on the floor. "Some other time."

Frank followed Jack's gaze to the bottle. "Yeah, sure Jack. Ben was alive but in terrible agony and pain. Maybe you felt bad for Ben, so you —"

"We'll talk later, detective. I can't think clearly right now. Later." Jack closed the door as Frank leaned in to press his inquiry. Jack leaned back against the door and slumped to the floor.

"Jack! Jack, can you hear me? I'm gonna leave my number. Call me. I'll be just across the street at the diner if you wanna talk. I think you'll feel much better after we talk some more. Jack? Jack, I'm just gonna slip my card here under the door. My number is right here under the door. Call me. Call me, Jack."

Frank and Vijay paused outside Jack's apartment building. "Frank, you think he is guilty? Why don't we take him to the station for more questions?"

"Don't got enough," said Frank. "But he did seem agitated. We stay on top of 'im."

Frank's phone buzzed in his pocket. "Yeah. Okay. Gimme twenty." To Vijay, "I can't wait for Wryder. I gotta go to the precinct. I'll catch a cab. Stay here and keep an eye on

Wryder. If he leaves, don't approach, but stay on 'im."

Vijay nodded, and Frank turned with a sigh, "And Vijay, if you follow Wryder, don't run 'im over."

Jack fumbled with the door lock and discovered the bolt didn't work. He grabbed the dusty wall phone and punched the keys for the building super. "Door latch doesn't work . . . No, I didn't break the lock . . . Don't know. Never used it . . . Hey, there's no need to get . . . That's right." Jack's stomach growled. "And hello? How's the food across the street?" *I think I'm hungry.*

---

The police captain took a huge bite out of the sandwich, leaned back in his chair, and mumbled through a mouthful, "Tell me about it, Frank."

"The one last night," Frank grimaced at the food rolling around in the captain's mouth, "Victim's name is Ben Fuller. Someone was seen outside the victim's room."

"And?"

"The hospital's chief pathologist, Jack Wryder, admitted to being in Fuller's room sometime that night. He was strung out. We're gonna keep tabs on 'im, maybe put a little pressure and then bring 'im in for more questions. The Medical Examiner expects to complete her initial report tomorrow."

"All right, Frank. Keep me informed. This one's special. Let me know what the M.E. finds and anything that might connect this guy, Wryder, to the other deaths."

There was a rap on the open door to the captain's office. A fresh-faced junior detective popped in. "Excuse me, Captain. Frank, Vijay's on your line."

Frank rose with an embarrassing squeak from the chair. "Thank you, Lowell," and excused himself to his desk, a push pin fabric cubicle in the busy bull pen outside the captain's office.

"What's up, Vijay?"

Vijay had called him from the car. "Wryder's standing outside the hospital."

"If he goes inside," said Frank, "get back here."


Jack marveled at how the hot dog vendor slathered on the brown mustard, sauerkraut, and onions sautéed with tomato paste. The vendor handed the hot dog to a customer, and without looking up, he dove into the steaming water to prepare another. He invited Jack, "Mustard and ketchup?"

"What he ordered," Jack pointed at the other customer who took a satisfying bite and walked away. "Make it two."

The vendor pressed the hot dog into Jack's hand without looking and prepared the second. The vendor handed him another. "Two more," asked Jack.

The vendor nodded and prepared two more. "Coke? Pepsi? Fanta?" He rummaged through the case of ice-buried cans and looked up at Jack. The hot dogs were gone. The vendor peered around his cart. No kids. The only evidence of the disappearing dogs was a dollop of mustard on Jack's lower lip and an avalanche of crumbs on his shirt.

"And one of those," Jack pointed to a large box of candy bars. The slogan on the box read "You're not you when you're hungry."

With the reassuring beeps of a healthy heart rhythm, the patient reclined in the hospital bed closest to the window and pulled the stiff sheet and blanket over his head. Raul had seen the patient's eyes, nostrils, lips, and ears appear reddened and flu-like. He tidied up the adjacent, unoccupied bed, and made his way over to open the window.

"Close it," snapped the patient. "It gets cold at night."

"Yes, sir." Raul closed the window but left it open the slightest crack. "I'll take care of you."

The pathology team changed from their lab clothes to civvies. It had been a long day for Jack, and he looked it. Sue stared at him. She had never seen Jack like this. He was disheveled and even a bit . . . smelly. Jack caught her spying him as he stuffed a large candy bar in his mouth.

Sue twisted her mouth. "Huh, I would have thought rice cakes. Actually, it may be the first time I've seen you eat anything. I was beginning to think you were some sort of . . ."

Jack froze — candy bar bulge in his cheek. *No way Sue suspects I'm a . . .*

"Health food nut. I imagine you eat rice cakes and granola," said Sue.

"Are they any good?" exhaled Jack, relieved.

"If you like eating plastic foam," said Kevin. "Come on Sue, let's go. We got our own eatin' to do." To Jack, "All those empty carbs'll kill you, buddy." Kevin and Sue exchanged a furtive glance and left together.

Tom put a warm hand on Jack's shoulder. "You look tired, Jack. You feel all right?"

"Yeah, I'm fine, Tom. First time I've slept in . . . Didn't sleep well last night."

"Well, I'm glad to see you leave on time, for once. Go home and relax. You work too hard. Tom gestured toward the long rows of drawers that contained the corpses, "You're beginning to look like one of them, Jack. Walk out with me."

"Go on ahead, Tom. I'm going to be a few minutes."

"Just a few?"

"Just a few. Good night, Tom."

"'Night Jack. Take tomorrow off. You need a break."

Jack listened to Tom's footsteps fade down the hall, and he locked the door to the noiseless room of corpses. *Dead* silence, mused Jack.

He rooted through his empty pockets before recalling that his pills had been lost down the drain. With a few uncertain steps, he approached the drawers, slid out a tray, and peeled back the sheet. He saw neither a spot of light above the head nor redness in the lifeless face. All the same, Jack cupped one hand and placed it palm down above the forehead of the corpse. He held his hand motionless. Nothing.

Jack swallowed hard and repositioned both of his hands above the forehead of the corpse. He closed his eyes. Seconds passed. A minute. An hour. Jack's hands trembled.

It was late, and Jack was the last person in the hospital cafeteria to be served hot food. The open seating area was already closed off to be cleaned, so Jack had to search among the plant-divided private spaces. He spotted Tracy behind a particularly large plant. She was hugging . . . *Sarah Ward?* Sarah gave Tracy a kiss on the forehead and left. Tracy settled down to a full tray of food.

As Jack advanced toward her, Tracy scooped up her tray. Her friend, Tina, had fed a steady flow of gossip into the hospital rumor mill after the night Ben Fuller died. Jack was a person of interest in the death of at least one patient. All that was once cute and quirky about Jack was now just plain creepy.

"Excuse me, Tracy. Was that Sarah Ward?"

"You know Sarah?" Tracy worked her way around Jack, avoiding eye contact.

"From the headlines," replied Jack. "I didn't know she worked here."

"She doesn't," Tracy spoke over her shoulder on the way to the exit. "She mentored me at Bellevue. Said she was here for an intervention. Sorry, Jack. Duty calls." And with a polite smile, she escaped. Jack found himself alone. Even the cleaning crew had left after roping off their work area.

"Jack," a voice called to him from within a bush. "Over here." White hair and clerical collar were enough for Jack to find a man seated behind a large cluster of potted plants.

"Is it Father?" asked Jack.

"Father, reverend, and once in England, rabbi," said the man pushing back an empty chair with his foot. "Please."

Jack took the seat and extended his hand. "Have we met?"

The man embraced Jack's hand in both of his. "You're no stranger to me, Jack. I've seen you visit the patients, and I've seen how you've touched many lives, particularly the children. I often visit the same people you do."

Jack drew a blank, and his face showed it.

"It's okay, Jack. Most people don't recognize me. I have a very forgettable face." The man's eyes were striking, compassionate, skin radiant for his age — an unforgettable face. He offered Jack a dinner roll. "What is it, Jack?"

"Bread."

"No," with an easy laugh the man asked again, "What is it, with *you*? You look troubled, Jack."

Jack felt an unfamiliar calm and spoke into his food. "If a person offends someone, betrays their trust, how do they make up for it?"

"The sincerity of our remorse for what we've done is the essential ingredient to earn forgiveness. Then we can begin the work to regain their trust. Redeeming ourselves is not as simple as being sorry, Jack." The man leaned in to catch Jack's eye. "But then the road to redemption is seldom an easy one."

*Redemption.* "Sorry," said Jack, "What was your —"

"Jack, the effort you make to be present for the people here at the hospital, your offer of comfort to the sick, the dying and their families — that's a good place for someone to start." Jack met the man's knowing gaze. "It is in our weakness," the man continued, "that the Almighty's power is greatest."

Jack was enraptured — for a moment. The speaker blared above his head, "The cafeteria is now closed. Please return your trays to . . ."

Jack rose from the table and thanked the chaplain. The chaplain placed a firm, compassionate hand upon Jack's arm.

"Don't be a stranger, Jack."

Jack nodded. Chin up, shoulders relaxed, he marched away with renewed purpose.

The plethora of stuffed animals was overwhelming. Jack had to make a choice before the gift shop closed. The attendant, whose kindness proved that not everyone was privy to hospital gossip, prepared to close for the night. Jack chose a small, white lamb.

"Emily," said Jack. "I'm going to spoil you."

"Would you like it wrapped?" asked the attendant with a hopeful look at the clock.

"No, thank you. I want to try and catch her before she's asleep."

On his way to Emily, muffled cries drew Jack toward another patient's room. In the privacy curtain, Jack saw a silhouette of a man hunched over the bed. There was something odd about it, and he stepped into the room for a closer look.

The patient monitor *buzzed* followed by the long beep of the flatline alarm. Jack groped for the light switch. As the lights flickered on, two nurses and an orderly rushed through the door. The privacy curtain rippled toward the window, and the silhouette was gone.

"Impossible," muttered Jack, his attention fixed on a thin opening in the window.

"He's not responding," shouted one of the nurses. "And the EKG . . . that suspicious tracing."

"It was murder. They were all killed," thought Jack aloud.

The orderly looked at Jack with wide eyes and slipped out of the room.

Jack examined the window. He ran his fingers along the narrow opening, and then slid it open wide to look down into the parking lot several floors below. The lot was cast in neat rows of light and shadow.

"What were you doing in here?"

Jack wanted to answer the nurse, but something odd in the lot below caught his eye.

"You're not on the duty schedule," the nurse swiped on her tablet.

"You don't understand," said Jack. "I was . . ." Something large scurried through the lot. Jack cupped his hands around his eyes to block the room's light. He managed to glimpse the silhouette he had seen earlier in the room. Behind Jack, the orderly had returned with a security guard, and the two crept toward him.

Anxious to get down to the lot below, Jack pivoted right into the barrel chest of the security guard. "Slow down, Doc," said the guard. "I just need to —" Jack brushed past the guard, who fell backward to the floor.

Jack bounded down a stairwell and exited the hospital into the parking lot. He ran to the area below the victim's room.

The stunned guard felt a lump under his back and pulled out a crushed toy lamb. "Anyone call the police?"

To Jack, the lot looked empty, but he was not alone. Someone, or something, lurked in a distant shadow, and with red-hued night-vision, tracked his every move.

Jack found an ID tag on the ground beneath the victim's window.

The orderly poked his head out of the window and pointed at Jack. "Down there. That's him! That's him!" A policeman appeared beside him and barked something into his radio.

Jack ran searching into the night.

"Jack?" Emily struggled to sit up at the sound of approaching footsteps. Her condition had deteriorated since Jack's last visit. Propped up on one elbow, she expected Jack to enter at any moment. After all, she believed, a pinky promise is the most powerful of promises.

Jack descended into the subway and shouldered his way into a car of sweaty passengers. The car bumped, squealed, and swayed as it raced through the dark tunnels. The inside of the car was bathed in red hues, and the whole suffocating atmosphere on the train conjured up an image of a descent into the bowels of Hell.

There were too many people, or too few seats, in the subway car. An elderly woman stood grasping the handrail above an oblivious, seated teenager. As the teen gathered up his backpack to depart at the next stop, a sharp dressed businessman stood close and tracked Jack's gaze from the open seat to the elderly woman. Then he maneuvered to take the seat.

"Really?" Jack gripped the arm of the businessman, who shrugged him off and took the seat anyway. Jack grabbed him by the lapels and pulled, intent on yanking him out of the seat. The man didn't budge. Jack realized he had overestimated his human strength.

"Oh Sh— " Jack uttered into a looming fist.

---

Forensic investigators scoured Jack's apartment. There was little to examine and even less light with which to examine it. The bedroom had a bed. A closet contained clothes. In the bathroom, hung a towel. And in the main room, two upholstered chairs, a floor lamp, a small potted tree, heavily-curtained windows, and one decoration on the wall — a small, framed photograph. Frank removed the photograph and held it in the light of the lamp. Two impeccably dressed male equestrians, about a thirty-year difference in age. Frank recognized the younger man in the photograph as Jack Wryder. The elder was a large man in his seventies, whose tame shadbelly coat contradicted the long, steel gray hair that hung wildly about his face. Frank handed the photo to an investigator. "Check if Wryder has any family in the area."

Vijay emerged from the bedroom closet, the beam of his new penlight darting between tiny slits in the back of a heavy, black vest. "He has body armor." Vijay brought the vest into the lamplight to show Frank. "And it took a few to the back."

"A stab vest," said Frank. "Not bullet proof. But it protects against knife attacks."

"So, Detective," an investigator drew Frank's attention from the vest, "What do you make of this? I'm still confused." He shook his head at a twisted, black skeleton of a tree potted beside one of the chairs.

"I saw it. Looks like one of my wife's plants. Wryder doesn't water his either."

"Not dehydrated. It's burned. Look closer. You can see that this isn't bark. It's charred. And, here at the base, ashes. There's an old electrical outlet here. I don't know. Maybe it threw a spark?"

With the end of a pen, Frank probed the soil. "Undisturbed ashes 'round the base. The tree burned right here." And looking up, "But there's no soot on the ceilin' or anywhere else." Frank pointed the tip of his pen at a smoke alarm.

*Screeech!* The subway car jolted to a stop, and Jack was jerked back to consciousness. The indifferent crowd of passengers filed past Jack to the open door. The elderly woman paused. She leaned down, patted Jack's head and whispered, "You could use this, sweetie." She tucked a small bottle of pepper spray inside his coat pocket.

Jack emerged from the subway stairwell across from his apartment into a carnival of flashing lights: red, white, yellow, and blue. Police cars crowded the street. The curtains in his apartment window were drawn apart, and inside, that chubby detective was reaching toward the ceiling. Jack clung to the wall. "I don't have time for this."

"You there! Stop!" a voice shouted up from the stairwell.

Jack froze. *Which was the better escape route? Streets or subway tunnels?* He peered down the stairwell. No police. A lone man in a long, dark, tattered overcoat tugged on the bill of his greasy baseball cap and extended his hand to Jack, "A dollar for food?"

Jack considered the police cars across the street. Two

officers emerged from one of the cars and turned toward him.

*Screeech!* The sound of the fire alarm from Jack's apartment diverted the officers' attention. Jack hurried back down the stairwell.

The smoke alarm startled everyone in the apartment. Well, except for Frank. All eyes were on him. Not satisfied with the smoke alarm's test button, Frank had ignited a page torn from his notebook and waved it above the charred remains of the potted tree. "Check with the neighbors if they heard a sound — like that one." The flames nibbled away at the final corner of the paper and Frank dropped it atop the pile of ash in the pot. He looked out the window. One second sooner and he would have seen Jack descend into the subway.

Something felt familiar about the destitute man, but Jack couldn't quite figure out what it was. He offered a few bills to the man. "Here. Here is that dollar for food, and this much more, and my coat, for those."

As they exchanged garments, the man seized Jack's hands. The power of the man's grip surprised Jack. "Thank you," the man stared into jack's eyes and rejoiced, "God bless you, man. I'll remember you. God bless you, man."

"Do I know you?" asked Jack, trying to turn his vague sense of the man into a concrete memory. Before the man could respond, voices echoed down the subway stairwell. *I've lingered too long*, thought Jack, and he hiked up the collar of the dark, tattered overcoat, pulled the filthy baseball cap low over his brow, and disappeared into one of the hundreds of tunnels snaking deep beneath the city.

The *plop, plop, plop* of dripping water suggested that the pitch-black area ahead was flooded. A torch was ignited and cast a brilliant light about the tunnel. But it would take a moment for the eyes to adjust. That's when the dragon attacked — to lethal effect.

"Shit!" exclaimed one of two pimply-faced desk clerks slumped behind the counter. "Double shit, dude," said the other. "You forgot to save the game before you died."

The dull *thunk* of the rusted reception desk bell got the clerks' attention, which was caught and held by the haunting, dark figure that stood before them.

"I need a room," Jack whispered.

Jack surveyed the squalid room. It was a low price to pay for a place to hide until he could figure out his next steps. He threw his coat and cap on the bed, entered the moldy-tiled bathroom, emptied his pockets onto the peeling laminate vanity, and took a shower in a vain attempt to wash away the events of the past few hours.

Jack had yet to rinse the soap from his eyes when the water ran ice cold. He toweled off, devoured a stale candy bar from the unplugged mini bar, and collapsed on the squeaky bed.

*There is a blinding light and a searing heat. Gabriel appears in angelic splendor. "You have committed offense against man and the Almighty. Stripped of all your powers. Repent. Save a hundred souls. Repent, Jack Wryder. Repent."*

Jack woke tangled in sweat-soaked sheets. He entered the bathroom to splash cold water on his face and glimpsed the image in the mirror. Curious. He was never interested in his face. It was somehow unfamiliar. Another, distorted, face was visible in the mirror. Atop the vanity lay the contents of his pockets, which included the ID tag he had found in the hospital parking lot.

*AMON.*

The reversed image of the name on the ID read "AMON LUAR." Jack swiped the tag off the counter and retrieved what passed as motel stationery – an eraserless half pencil and yellowed note pad. Jack copied the name from the ID onto the pad: "RAUL NOMA."

Raul Noma? Jack recalled how Emily had been terrified of the hospital orderly. Jack tore the sheet off the pad and rushed out of the room.

"Excuse me," whispered Jack, startling one of the Clerks off his chair.

"Whoa. Sorry, sir. Problem with the room?"

Jack nodded toward the computer. "You online?"

"Yeah. Sorry. We're just playing —"

"I need a quick search on a name," said Jack.

"Just gimme a sec and we'll switch out." The clerks exited the game.

Jack attempted to squeeze around the reception desk to the terminal, but the tight space behind the counter was littered with empty cans, gaming magazines, and pizza boxes.

"Uhm, not much room back here, just give us the name you wanna search up."

"Amon." Jack read the letters on the pad in reverse, "A-M-O-N."

As the clerks tapped away on the computer, Jack leaned back against the counter and faced the cluttered reception area: a few thickly upholstered chairs clustered around a water-stained coffee table; faded velvet wallpaper; a big old boxy television set mounted on the wall flashing muted images of his face; curtains with . . . *Wait what?*

On the television screen, the news ticker flashed: "Special: Mystery Murders," above it, an unflattering hospital ID photo with the boldly printed name, WRYDER, Jack S. There was an offer of a cash award for information leading to his arrest.

"Weird. Where'd you get the name?" asked one of the clerks.

Jack snapped his neck around and met the clerk's eyes. The clerk glanced away toward the computer screen. "That all?" asked the clerk. "For the search?"

"Yes. Please." Jack shifted his body to block the clerks' view of the television.

"I'm just looking," Jack noted the gaming magazines and fantasy regalia that littered the area behind the desk, "for a cool character name."

"Hey man, you seriously a gamer?" Both clerks turned expectant to Jack.

"Writer," said Jack, gesturing toward the computer to divert the clerks' away from the television. "I'm a writer. Any hits?"

"Oh, right." One of the clerks mumbled off the list of search results.

"Stop," Jack rapped a knuckle on the counter. "Read that

one."

"Amon. Amon is a demon identified in Collin de Plan-cy's Dic-tion-nair-e Infer-nal. With some initial stumbling over the words, the clerks read the online description of "Amon." They soon adopted a dramatic narrator's tone as the passage captured their imagination. "Reginald Scot records in his Discovery of Witchcraft written in 1584: 'Amon or Aamon, is a great and mightie marques, and commeth abroad in the likenes of a woolfe, having a serpents taile, spetting out and breathing flames of fier; when he putteth on the shape of a man, he sheweth out dogs teeth, and a great head like to a mightie raven; he is the strongest prince of all others, and understandeth of all things past and to come, he procureth favor, and reconcileth both freends and foes, and ruleth fourtie legions of divils.'"

"Awesome," the clerks shook with excitement. "Great choice for a champion. Hey man," the clerks looked up, "what do think about . . . ?"

Jack was gone.

The clerks peered over the counter at the floor and scanned the reception area. They found him. There was Jack, on the television, full screen, below the caption, "Angel of Death."

"Oh shit," said one clerk to the other.

"Double shit, dude."

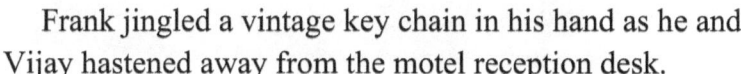

Frank jingled a vintage key chain in his hand as he and Vijay hastened away from the motel reception desk.

"What do you make of it, Frank?"

"Well, I don't think he's a writer," replied Frank. "Maybe lookin' up an old friend — someone Wryder trusts."

Lowell was waiting for the detectives outside the closed door to Jack's room. Frank and Vijay approached him, and Lowell gestured that someone was in the room. A shadow shifted in the light beneath the door. Frank, Vijay, and Lowell drew their guns and formed-up outside the room. Frank quietly slid the key into the lock and counted out with his fingers. *One, two . . .*

The key turned. The lock *clicked.*

*. . . three.*

Frank and Vijay burst through the doorway.

"Aiee!" screamed the housekeeper, seeking refuge behind the bed.

"Damn it," Frank gestured for the others to lower their weapons. "Damn it to Hell."

The terrified housekeeper trembled beside the bed and began to gather up the trash and her meager cleaning supplies. Frank figured there might be something useful in the mess.

"Leave those here. Nothin', but you, leaves this room," said Frank. And to Vijay, "See if Wryder left us more than lookin' like idiots."

While Frank and Vijay searched the room, Lowell retrieved their messages from the precinct. "Wryder's phone was tracked to a homeless man, who was also wearing Wryder's coat. He didn't know he had the phone."

Frank found the motel stationary pad and pencil. He examined the pad and rubbed the pencil across the surface of the paper. "Now who do you suppose that is?"

Frank handed the rubbing to Lowell. "Run a check on that name, Raul Noma."

Jack hid his face as police cruisers rolled past the street-side phone kiosk. "You sure?" Jack spoke at the Link phone's touch screen. "That's spelled N-O-M-A."

"I'm sorry, sir." Replied the operator. "There is no residence listing for a Raul Noma, last name spelled N-O-M-A, in that district either."

Jack swipe closed the screen and scanned the street. A city bus rolled by with Memorial Hospital's public health advertisement — high-cheekboned physician, four-foot-wide cheesy smile, and the line, "We have the answers."

# Five

FRANK HAD NOT GOTTEN USED TO BRIEFING the captain directly. And mindful of the tiny squeals of the chair straining beneath his heft, Frank was less animated than he often needed to fully express himself.

"Frank, you've got Wryder's apartment staked out as well as the motel. And we have extra patrolmen at the hospital. What else do you need to bring this guy in?"

"I need forensics to go back through all the earlier deaths and take a fresh look at the evidence. This time, assume an expert in pathology is involved. I need more to connect Wryder to these deaths."

"Okay, Frank. But you bring him in, and let's wrap this up. Wryder's our man. Your report. Witnesses place him at the scenes of two possible homicides. And he's running."

Frank leaned forward, as much as the groaning chair would safely permit. "Wryder's a pathologist. He'd know how to conceal the cause of death. But it just doesn't feel right. Of the two deaths we connect with Wryder, Ben Fuller is different. All the other victims got a known criminal history or seriously deviant behavior. All seven of —"

"Careful, Frank. Only three *official*."

"All three of the *known* victims were freakin' evil people. Our killer's profile is some sort of vigilante — targetin' people accused or convicted of some awful shit. But Ben Fuller lived the life of a saint."

"Maybe Wryder made a mistake when he killed Ben Fuller. Or maybe Wryder knew something about Fuller that your team missed. Fuller might not be the saint you think he was."

"All right, Captain. A guy buys a stuffed animal to give to a little girl and on the way decides, hey, maybe I'll take a few minutes to off someone. Toys for tots and a mercy killing — all in a day's work."

"Come on, Frank. Give me a break. Since when did you care if any of the guys you collared made sense? His coworkers say he drives himself to exhaustion. He's tired, has no friends, and likely delusional. Your team found empty pill bottles in his apartment. He's on something. Who knows what? Maybe he wanted to get caught this time. Bring this guy in, Frank. Wryder's our man, and he'll crack when you question him here."

"I ain't saying we don't got enough evidence for the DA to make a case."

The captain leaned forward in his chair — noiseless Frank noted — and pointed at him. "Get him, Frank. Your assignment is clear. Bring in Wryder, or I'll get someone else to do it." Then he reclined and relaxed into a saccharine smile. "How's the Pakistani working out?" He thumbed toward Vijay who paced outside the office.

"Vijay? Good. And he's Indian not Pakistani. But . . ."

"That's fine, Frank, fine."

"But it would be best if I were behind the wheel for the rest of his tour. Let 'im play bumper cars with the Feds."

"I made a commitment, Frank. He doesn't need to qualify for NASCAR."

"Yeah, but —"

The captain made a show of picking up the phone, "Good day, Frank."

Vijay waited for Frank outside the captain's office. Among the clamor of the busy precinct, Vijay spoke to Frank in an unnecessarily low voice, "You were arguing with the captain? Was it my car accident? Am I in trouble?"

"It's pretty bad," Frank whispered back. "He suggested that I drive for a while, just until things settle down in the mayor's office."

"The mayor?"

"Shh. Keep it down. Let's keep this between you and me, partner. We'll work through it together."

"Frank!" Lowell called from across the room, "Frank!" The exuberant detective wound his way through the office waving a large manila envelope.

"Easy Lowell. Take a breath. Whatcha got there?"

Lowell handed Frank the envelope, from which Frank removed a photocopied image of Raul.

"Raul Noma," proclaimed Lowell. "He works at the same hospital as your Jack Wryder. Do you think he's helping Wryder?" Laughter and jeers erupted in the crowded office behind them. Frank turned to see what all the fuss was about.

Unfurled from the ceiling was a large poster. It was a life-size photo of Frank, half-crouched atop a table, completely disheveled, his face beet red, and a vent cover hung about his waist like a hula skirt.

"Hey Frank," cried an anonymous voice from the crowd of detectives and uniformed officers, "you wanna talk about what went on in there? In the big … dark … scary vent."

Frank walked out of the office and flipped off the room over his shoulder. "Vijay, let's head over to Memorial and find out if Mr. Noma's been contacted by our friend, Dr. Wryder." The laughter rose behind Frank as he and Vijay left the precinct.

There was a visible police presence outside the busy entrance to Memorial Hospital. Jack watched from across the street, careful to keep the sunlight glinting off the skyscrapers at his back. He draped the old overcoat over his arm, removed his cap, clipped his hospital ID onto his shirt pocket and entered a side alley. A few hospital workers smoked, vaped, and otherwise ignored Jack walking past and through the emergency door, which was propped open with a brick.

Jack glanced at his watch and peeked through the door of the basement stairwell. Kevin groped and Sue giggled their way down the corridor and into the elevator. Jack took a wary step through the doorway.

"Hold it!"

Jack ducked behind the door as Tom emerged from the morgue and ran toward him. Tom exhaled, "Thanks for holding it, guys. Where you two headed for lunch?"

A jolly secretary chatted away on a telephone headset. "Wow-wee. Sounds like you guys had a really fun time. The phone beeped an incoming call. The call ID read "Pathology."

"I'm sorry, Marge. It's an internal call. I'll call you back." She punched a button, "Administrator's Office, how can I help you?" Her eyes grew wide. "Oh, my goodness."

On the other end of the line, Jack was on the phone inside the morgue. "Our team wanted to send Raul condolences and . . ." A bright red apple lay on the counter. "And fruit to his home. But we don't know where to send it."

Frank and Vijay entered the administrator's office as the secretary typed up the search for Raul's address. "That is so thoughtful of you guys," she continued on the phone with Jack.

Frank leaned in. "Excuse me. Detective Frank Kelly to meet with . . ." The secretary held a palm to Frank's face.

"Okay, here we are. Raul Noma, 69 125th Street, Apartment 4B."

Frank was confused. "How did ya' know we wanted to speak with Mr. Noma?"

"I wasn't speaking to *you*, sir. Raul's brother passed, and I was getting his address for a colleague." To Jack, "I'm sorry, sir. I was interrupted by . . ." Frank looked at the call ID.

"Pathology!" Frank barked into his radio. "He's in the morgue."

". . . a very rude policeman. Shall I read the address again?"

Frank and Vijay burst through the doorway. Lowell emerged from the locker room. "Nobody in here." The telephone receiver dangled from the wall.

Frank growled into his radio, "Tell me the exits are covered. Tell me the exits are covered!"

Vijay left the morgue, but Frank lingered a moment to glance around the room one final time, from the door of the morgue to the wall across the room, and along the row of

58

identical drawers that contained the corpses.

The cold fog of Jack's breath glowed in a narrow shaft of light, and he shifted his bodyweight atop the lumpy surface. Corpses, Jack discovered, make poor pillows.

After Frank left the room, it had grown quiet enough for Jack to risk opening the door and begin the slide out of the drawer. The chill had penetrated his bones, and even the airconditioned air of the morgue would be a welcome respite.

*Crash!* The morgue doors swung wide open against the walls. Jack withdrew into the drawer and pulled the door closed, leaving a gap wide enough to permit him a glimpse of three NYPD-blue uniforms. The older of the three officers barked, "Wait here until CSI arrives. Nobody touches the phone, or anything else, until CSI is finished. Think you rookies can handle it?"

"Yes, Sergeant," they replied in unison as the sergeant left the morgue.

It wasn't long before the young cops grew bored. They fidgeted with the gear on their utility belts while they waited for the crime scene investigators to arrive. One of them nodded toward the drawers.

"Dude, you think they got bodies?"

"Yeah. Probably. It's a morgue."

"Take a look."

"Why me?"

"You're closer."

"We're not supposed to touch anything."

"They only want the phone for prints. Don't be a wuss."
He walked over to one end of the long row of drawers and opened the first drawer in the row. He reached inside the

drawer to slide out the tray. It was empty.

"Maybe they're all empty. Come on. It's not worth it."

He waved off his partner and opened the next drawer, "Winner!" He pulled out the drawer and drew back the sheet that covered the body. "Whoa, this guy's a prune."

The other cop peeked over but kept his distance across the room. "Come on. We're gonna get caught."

"Relax." He closed the drawer and opened the next one. "Whoa, this babe must've been a knockout. What a set of . . ." *Creeek*. Now the other cop had begun to open the drawers. The cops, one on either end of the row, converged on Jack, opening the drawers one by one, some empty, others with corpses.

Each of Jack's anxious breaths glowed in the thin light. The sound of the drawers, opening and closing, grew louder as they closed in on him. The light disappeared in a shadow. Both cops reached for Jack's drawer at the same time.

"After you."

One of the cops grasped the handle and pulled open the door. Jack could smell the new leather of the cop's utility belt and read the patent number on the grip of his pistol. A hairy, reaching hand brushed Jack's cheek.

"What's going on?" asked Tom. He stood in the morgue doorway, hands on his hips. The two cops froze, like deer in the headlights.

The view from inside the drawer rapidly narrowed. Jack inserted his finger in the opening before the door could lock shut. The steel door crushed his finger, and Jack bit his lip to keep silent.

"Uh," the cop leaned back heavily on the drawer door.

"We were just . . ."

". . . waiting for CSI to arrive," said the other cop. "You had a break-in. Don't touch anything." He gestured to the crime scene investigators who at that moment entered the room. "CSI will take it from here." The two rookie cops shuffled past Tom and out of the morgue.

Jack freed his finger and examined it in the dim light of the drawer. It was already beginning to swell. Jack held the throbbing finger against the chilled metal lining of the drawer. Outside, Tom and the crime scene investigators exchanged a few words — inaudible above the chatter of his teeth.

Frank and Vijay lounged in the hospital administrator's spacious, warmly paneled office. The administrator handed each of the detectives a fresh cup of hot coffee. "Raul Noma has been with us about seven months. Dr. Wryder joined us about a week after Raul started."

As if on cue, Raul crept into the room. His pale complexion was a few shades lighter than his faded scrubs. The detectives struggled to rise from deeply cushioned chairs, and the hospital administrator introduced Raul. "Thank you for coming on such short notice, Raul. I'm sure you are very busy." Raul approached, wary of the two men.

"These are Detectives Kelly and Vashi," said the administrator.

Frank offered his hand, "Good afternoon, Mr. Noma."

Raul simply nodded.

The administrator cleared her throat. "Raul, the police are interested in what you know about —"

"Thanks for the introduction," Frank interjected. "We just got a few questions, Mr. Noma, about your relationship with another employee here at the hospital. How well do you know Jack Wryder?"

"Dr. Wryder? Not much. He works in the morgue, right?"

"Has Dr. Wryder contacted you recently? Anytime in the past day or two?"

Raul shook his head. "Last time I saw him was here. At the hospital. Just passing."

"Do you share any mutual friends with Dr. Wryder?"

"Not that I know of."

"Can ya' think of any reason why he would want to try and contact you?"

"No. Why?"

"Wryder wrote the name, Raul Noma, on a . . . Are ya' sure ya' can't think of why he might want to contact you?"

"I don't know. Am I the only Raul Noma in the city?"

Vijay cocked his head to the side. "I am very sorry about your brother." At which Raul gave a puzzled look. "Your brother passed away recently, yes?" asked Vijay.

"That's not possible," said Raul.

"Why not?" said Frank.

"Because I don't have a brother."

"Wryder attempted to obtain your home address," said Frank. "He wanted to send fruit to your home."

"Fruit?"

"Don't you worry, Mr. Noma," said Frank with a sideways glance at Vijay. "We'll keep an eye on your apartment — in case Dr. Wryder does try and contact you."

Raul squirmed and crossed his arms. "Is that really

necessary?"

Frank raised an eyebrow. Raul adopted a more conciliatory tone, "I mean, do I have a reason to fear Dr. Wryder?"

"We don't think so," said Frank. "But if Wryder does contact you, or if ya' can remember any reason why he might be trying to contact you, please gimme a call." Frank gave Raul his card and noticed the word "TEMPORARY" printed on Raul's ID tag. Frank gestured toward the tag. "Lose your tag?"

"Huh? No. Probably misplaced it. It'll turn up. Always does."

The hospital administrator escorted Frank and Vijay out of her office. Raul hesitated and stroked his ID tag.

Jack took shallow breaths and stopped shivering — he was hypothermic. At least an hour had passed since the CSI team wrapped up their work, but the pathology team had been permitted to return. Now, muted music played through the narrow opening in the drawer as Sue, dressed in scrubs, tidied up around the tables and lab benches. Tom and Kevin emerged from the locker room, dressed to leave for the day.

"All these policemen around," Tom shook his head. "It has to be stressful for the patients and staff."

"I'm cool with it," said Kevin. "It's for our protection too."

"You can't be serious," said Tom. "What kind of danger are we in?"

"Look, the sooner Jack is caught the sooner it can all get back to normal 'round here."

"Get back to normal? We don't know that Jack had

anything to do with these deaths."

"Murders, Tom. Murders, not deaths. Let's call 'em what they are. And, if Jack's so innocent, how come he's runnin' from the cops? Also, Jack has been obsessed 'bout the so-called "suspicious" deaths." Kevin looked at Sue. "He's on somethin'. I've seen him slip a bottle of pills in and out of his pocket."

Sue's eyes widened like saucers. "No. Really?"

"Sure. I mean, whadda we know 'bout him? Other than what you see here at the hospital, whaddya know about Jack?"

"I guess he has been acting a little odd lately," Sue conceded.

Tom gaped at Sue. "What, you too?"

"I don't know, Tom. I don't want to believe that Jack is a . . . could harm anyone."

"In any case," said Tom. "I do believe Jack should turn himself in and clear things up."

"On that point we agree," said Kevin, and he opened the morgue door for Tom.

Tom thanked Sue for picking up the extra work. "It's the big game. I honestly didn't think her team would make it this far. I'll pick up the workload tomorrow."

"Yeah, I'll *pitch-in* too," Kevin added with a knowing glance to Sue. "Now don't work too hard."

With Sue alone in the room, Jack felt safe to begin his escape from the drawer. But before he could slide out, Kevin returned and locked the door.

Sue snapped off her gloves, cranked up the music, and passionately embraced Kevin. Deftly with one hand, Kevin lowered the height of a gurney behind Sue, and they fell hard upon it. The gurney glided toward Jack, bumped the door of his drawer, and then came to a stop just a few feet away. Kevin and Sue made noisy love.

Jack seized the opportunity to make his escape. He slid out of the drawer on the tray, which paralleled the lovers' gurney, and rolled himself off the corpse.

Kevin kissed Sue's body, working his way down from her neck. She arched her back atop the gurney and sensing a presence opened her eyes — face to face with a corpse.

The scream was deafening.

Jack, alone and soaked in cold sweat, was roused by the jerk and screeching halt of the subway car. He crossed over from the station, navigating the busy street, and ducked into an alley to avoid a passing patrol car. He peered around the corner.

The patrol car slowed and betrayed Detective Lowell who was staked outside the motel in an unmarked car. Jack backed up toward the subway entrance across the busy street, his attention remained fixed on the detective. Gabriel's voice boomed in Jack's head, *"Your soul is what they need."*

*Beep! Beep!* Horns *blared* and brakes *squealed* as cars swerved to avoid Jack.

Lowell marked Jack and radioed for backup.

Jack refocused and sprinted to the subway entrance but was pushed back by a wave of people bustling up the steps. He abandoned the subway and raced down the street. Lowell led the foot chase joined by two uniformed cops. Jack dashed across the street, and one step from the curb he was struck to the ground. Jack stumbled onto the sidewalk and into the laughing face of a pimply-faced twenty-something standing on a . . . *wheel*? Jack knocked him off the Segway and sped off down the sidewalk.

Bent over and winded, Lowell looked after Jack in disbelief. "Wryder's turned the corner from Lexington Avenue," he called into his radio. "Now heading west on East 73rd Street. He's riding a . . . a wheel."

Jack took the next turn down a dark alley, whizzed through it, and onto another sidewalk. Dodging pedestrians and the debris which littered the sidewalk, he jumped the curb and landed in the street.

Police sirens blared, and Jack glanced over his shoulder. A trail of police cars twisted toward him through heavy traffic.

*Thwap!* Jack's whole body was slapped hard from behind by the wind of a passing truck. And though he narrowly avoided a fatal collision, the turbulence rocked the self-balancing Segway and forced Jack to slow down. As he rebalanced, Jack caught a glimpse of the driver that had nearly killed him — a demonic figure — distorted through the window glass.

The patrol cars closed the distance to Jack. "He's heading south on Park Avenue," radioed one of the drivers. "Just passing 70th Street."

"Stay on 'im." Frank responded. "We're headed north on Madison. I'll cut 'im off."

Jack swerved down a narrow side street. The patrol car was now close enough behind him that Jack could hear the growl of its engine. "Pull over," blared from the patrol car speakers, "and stop your . . . stop."

Frank and Vijay's car turned the corner and into Jack's path. Jack was trapped between the patrol cars.

"Got 'im," Frank grinned like the Cheshire Cat. "Hang on Vijay. I'll show you how to drive."

Frank's car screeched and smoked as it cut ninety-degrees sideways. Jack ground to a stop within an inch of the car and slowly tipped forward; his belt buckle kissed the car with a click. Then Jack pivoted away and sped off, hopping the curb onto the sidewalk.

The patrol cars behind Jack attempted to stop, but the momentum of the lead car carried it screeching into the side of Frank's car. The rest of the cars piled up behind.

Jack, the loose strap of his baseball cap flapping in the breeze, whizzed down another alley, rolling past a homeless woman who hobbled along in the darkness. He glanced over his shoulder.

Frank paced in the flashing lights of the tow trucks and other emergency vehicles that tended the pile of patrol cars. He spoke on the phone while Vijay watched the tow crews untangle the mess. "Shit," Frank pocketed his phone. "We lost 'im."

Lowell, whom Frank had begun to count on to appear out of nowhere, shouted, "He was spotted outside Central Park at East 66th Street, heading south on Fifth Avenue."

"Bingo," exclaimed Frank. "Let's move."

Frank, Vijay, Lowell, and all the officers piled into the few cars that were spared significant damage. Frank and Vijay squeezed into a back seat together. Lights flashing and sirens blaring, they peeled out down the street.

Frank spotted the Segway first. Slower than before, the wheel and its driver headed down a poorly lit sidewalk. Frank and Vijay were crowded in the back of a patrol car, faces pressed against the bullet proof divider. They strained to see out the front window. Frank commanded the driver, "Tell 'em to cut off Wryder at 61st. We're gonna drive 'im straight toward 'em." Frank shook his head. "And what the hell is that thing?" he asked rhetorically.

"A Segway Ninebot One," replied Vijay. "Electric one wheel self-balancing transporter. But," with a wobble of his head, "they are no longer manufactured. And that one is much fas— "

"Okay, Einstein," Frank placed a silencing hand on Vijay's shoulder. "Wryder turned down a blind alley. This is it."

The Segway crawled down a narrow alley that widened at the end into a circular space that formed a sort of dead-end amphitheater of trash cans. The patrol cars filed down the alley and maneuvered around the edges of the amphitheater to block the only exit. Pistol slides were racked, and spotlights converged to stage-light the back of their target. Before his car had even stopped, Frank bound out of it like a child on Christmas morning.

"Oh, we got you. No. *I* got you," crowed Frank. "I got you!" He pushed forward through a firing line of officers. In one hand, Frank's handcuffs dangled, sparkling in the lights, in the other he sighted his pistol on the back of Jack's filthy baseball cap. "End of the line, Wryder," he shouted at the figure huddled beneath the old, tattered overcoat. "Hands up. Turn around. Slowly."

As the rider turned, Frank glimpsed bedraggled hair. Slender, wrinkled hands emerged. Frank's eyes narrowed. "No."

The former actress turned into the bright lights and greeted her audience with a wide, toothless grin. She removed the cap, bowed slightly, and squinted, searching the lights for that handsome man to whom she had to thank for this cozy old coat and the performance of her life. A *thunderclap* concluded the show.

Jack sought shelter from the violent cloudburst and lightning beneath an overpass in Central Park. He had given away his coat to the homeless woman, and he was soaked to the bone. After hours of hiding inside the morgue drawer, the excitement of his escape from the police had offered some relief from the cold. But the adrenaline rush faded, and Jack's energy and mood crashed along with his body temperature. His colleagues could not be trusted to help him. Cold and alone, Jack was mentally and physically depleted.

The sight of flashlights in the distance drove Jack deeper into the dark tunnel where he felt safe enough to close and rest his eyes.

"Sauriel."

Out of the darkness, a chilling, inhuman voice exhaled,

"Sauriel."

Jack shuffled in the dark to face the voice.

"We've been a bad little angel, haven't we?"

Jack groped in the dark. *Which direction was the voice coming from?*

"I can use someone like you down here."

"Who are you?" Jack stumbled. "What do you want?"

"You have already given me what I want, *Jack*. Your corrupted soul." The voice was louder, corporeal, and close to Jack. "Release it to me!"

Jack felt powerful wings sweep across the back of his neck. He lurched out of the tunnel and fell to the ground. The rain had stopped.

Jack waited for the attack that never came. As he rose to his feet and turned out his mud-soaked pockets, a torn-out newspaper article fell to the ground.

Across the street and above a doorway, a neon sign buzzed: "Shelter", "All Are Welcome." Evocative of the night he stalked Sarah Ward, Jack found he had come full circle. He crossed over and entered the shelter.

Gideon sat behind a small desk and punched away on an old computer. Tiny half-frame reading glasses perched incongruously atop his meaty nose. Jack sized up the room — fluorescent lights cast a pale green hue over bare folding tables, metal chairs, and concrete floors. Gideon's voice boomed, "The Ritz is a short ride and a few-hundred bucks away."

"I don't know," said Jack. "I expected . . ."

"Less gray? Have a seat and make yourself comfortable."
Gideon gestured toward a metal folding chair. "Your name?"

"I only need a place for tonight."

"We need your name and some basic information. It's the
law, man. That's all."

A lizard-faced man lurked behind two heavy metal fire
doors, an unlit cigarette dangling from his lips. His eyes were
fixed on Jack as he flicked a lighter. Gideon pointed a finger
at the smoker. It might as well have been a gun barrel. "Hey,
man. You know better. Take it outside." Smoker grumbled
under his breath and left. Gideon turned back to Jack.
"Name?"

"John. John Smith."

"John? Smith?" Gideon peered over his glasses. "Is John
Smith a U.S. citizen?"

From an adjoining room, Sarah emerged. She was a spot
of vibrant color in the pallid room.

Jack immediately regretted his decision to come to the
shelter. He was sure that Sarah would recognize him from the
night he had followed her. Sarah picked through a pile of
paperwork on the desk, and without acknowledging Jack's
presence, she addressed the actual elephant in the room.
"Gideon."

"Yes, Ms. Ward."

"After you complete the interview and give him his
assistance number, send him in. I'll do the orientation."

Gideon escorted Jack into Sarah's office and handed her a
file, proclaiming, "Mr. John Smith." Soaked and scruffy, Jack

was a mere vestige of the powerful figure that Sarah had confronted a few nights ago.

Sarah thanked Gideon, who proffered a mock bow as he withdrew from the room. "Have a seat, Mr. *Smith*. My name is Sarah. I like to get to know the people who will stay with us."

"Only tonight. I'm not staying."

"Only tonight? What about tomorrow night? And the next? We have services that may help you."

"Help me? No. No, thank you."

Sarah cocked her head and squinted. "Have we met before?"

Jack met Sarah's penetrative gaze and shook his head. "I don't think so."

"Are you sure?"

"No, I'm sure of it." His shoulders tightened. "We've never met."

"I'm sorry to be such a pest. I'm normally quite good at remembering faces. Especially the handsome ones."

"Hmm." It was an obvious attempt to win him over. Nonetheless, under the circumstances Jack was flattered, and he relaxed his shoulders.

"Well then, let's set you up. I'll give you the quick tour and allow you to get that one night's sleep. Gideon is always around somewhere if you require assistance." Sarah stuffed Jack's file into her desk drawer. Pill bottles rattled around inside the drawer, and Jack appeared to notice.

"You have a coat?" exclaimed Sarah. The volume of her voice surprised her as much as it did Jack. Before Jack could respond, Sarah dragged over a large cardboard box from the corner of the room. "No?" she opened the box. "You can take one from here."

Inside the box, Jack found a heavy, black oilskin drover, which bore a remarkable resemblance to the one he had exchanged with the destitute man in the subway. In fact, he was pretty sure that this was *his* coat.

Jack settled with a squeak onto the camp bed — one of dozens of identical cots arranged in neat rows spanning the full length and width of a large gymnasium. Moonlight spilled in through windows high up on the walls. Jack closed his eyes in peace and drifted off to sleep. The balled-up paper upon which he had written Raul's address rolled out of his loosened fist.

Inside the precinct's interview room, Vijay and Lowell flanked Smoker, who was slouched across the table from Frank. Smoker fondled a photograph with his tobacco-stained fingers and coughed, "That's him — the angel of death guy on the news. Where's my reward?"

"You're sure that's the man you saw last night?" asked Frank. "At the shelter?"

Jack walked tall down the street — long, black overcoat flowing around him — renewed by his visit to the shelter. He caught a look at his formidable reflection in the uneven glaze of a bagel shop's plate glass window. What was it Mrs. Lopez had called him, Santa Muerte? An Angel of Death.

Jack matched Raul's address on the note paper to an overhead street sign. A block ahead, there was a pair of uniformed policemen posted outside of Raul's building. He scanned the area from the policemen up to the floor of Raul's apartment and across to the roof of the adjacent building. I'll need supplies, thought Jack.

Jack clambered up the fire escape taking great care not to drop the brown paper bag which was stretched to its breaking point. He reached the roof of the building across from Raul's apartment and peered over the edge of the low wall. A policeman fidgeting with his phone moved through the alley below. Jack sized up the distance across the alley to the rooftop of Raul's building. Then he carefully opened the bag and spilled out the contents: a mound of candy bars and juice boxes. Jack reclined against the wall with his supplies. Behind him, the late afternoon sun streamed reds and yellows through the city skyline.

Among the litter of empty candy wrappers and crushed juice boxes, Jack peered over the edge of the roof into the gray alley below. A patrol car had entered the alley and was idling at the far end. The policeman who was posted in the alley walked toward the car. He held out a hand to shield his eyes from the blaring headlights.

Jack seized the opportunity. He had estimated the distance across the alley and stepped back several feet. He inhaled, crouched, leaned forward, sprinted to the edge, and slipped.

Jack fell short. He barely cleared his chest and arms over the roof gutter, and his legs dangled above the alley. His foot had slipped as he launched himself off the roof and into the air.

The policeman returned below Jack with a fresh cup of coffee in hand when the gutter above him rattled. He glanced up at the edge of the roof from which Jack had leapt. Jack managed to pull the rest of his body up and over onto the opposite rooftop. The policeman's eyes swept across to where Jack had clung a moment ago. Nothing.

Jack collapsed on the roof. A silvery ribbon fluttered from beneath his shoe. He had lost traction because of a slippery candy bar wrapper that had stuck to the sole of his shoe. Kevin was right, Jack recalled, *those carbs can kill you.* Jack waited for the policeman in the alley to settle in with the inevitable distraction of his phone, then he snuck down a fire escape and through an open window into Raul's apartment.

*Yowl!* Hackles raised, a black cat howled and hissed at Jack. Its mangy fur resembled its owner's greasy coif. Jack pulled a candy bar from his pocket and tossed it at Raul's cat. "Nice evil kitty."

He began with the kitchen, searching the drawers, closets, and cabinets. Except for several freshly baited rodent traps, like the drawers and closets, Jack found all the cabinets empty.

Frank and Vijay cruised down the street toward the homeless shelter in their new car. The radio crackled to life. "NYPD we have a 10-10 P at 69 125th Street. Building super reports tenants saw a man climb down a fire escape and enter an open window."

"125th Street," Frank pointed at the radio. "That's Raul

Noma's."

"3 Adam 84, we're at the scene."

"3 Adam, the super will meet you at main entrance and let you inside."

"10-4."

Frank and Vijay peeled out toward 125$^{th}$ street.

Buzzing flies drew Jack's attention to the refrigerator. Cockroaches joined their flying cousins around the nozzle of the water dispenser. A drop of bright red liquid oozed from the nozzle's tip. Jack slowly opened the refrigerator door.

A severed ram's head, upon which a five-pointed star had been drawn in fresh blood, stared dully at Jack from the otherwise empty fridge. An elaborately ornamented dagger protruded from the head. Jack pried the dagger loose and examined the most striking feature of the ornamentation: a green pentagram formed of inlaid gemstones. *Not quite emerald or jade, but perhaps* . . . Jack froze. Raul appeared behind him.

Jack, already armed with the dagger in hand, turned slowly to strike a confident pose. "It was you," Jack pointed the dagger at Raul. "You knew their souls were at risk. You killed those patients before their souls could be saved. You're the demon, Amon."

Raul stepped back, grinning, "Wow. Quite a story, Dr. Wryder. You have some imagination. You break into my apartment, and then you accuse me of being a murderer. And what was it? A demon? Too much time spent down there in the morgue. You're a pathologist, not an . . ." Raul regarded Jack's grim expression and lost his grin. "Jack *Sauriel*

Wryder. Sauriel, The Releaser."

"I am."

"Huh," Raul shook his greasy mane, "I am surprised I didn't see it before. Although, I did find it amusing. A human, in the morgue, bearing the name of one of the angels of death." Raul pointed to the dagger in Jack's hand. "I'm no danger to your kind. With a simple gesture you have the power to send my soul back. But remember this: I will return to this world — not as Raul — maybe Bob, Barbara, or perhaps . . . Emily."

*If* I had the power, Jack thought to himself, and he handed the dagger to Raul. "You are no danger to me," Jack bluffed. "Send yourself back. Avoid the agony I'm tempted to cause you."

"Oh, you are an angel, Sauriel, to spare me the pain of my soul ripped from this living, human body." Raul placed the tip of the blade tight against his own throat.

*Meooow!*

Jack glanced at the screaming cat. Raul glanced at an open window — and he was gone.

Jack looked out the window and saw Raul running through the alley below. He climbed out the window and slid down the fire escape. He chased Raul into a blind alley without windows or any other route of escape.

Raul backed up into the shadow of the darkest corner, where with red-hued night vision he could clearly see Jack. Jack was walking up the alley, straight toward him.

Jack's eyes seemed fixed on Raul. Then he stopped abruptly and looked away. Jack scanned the dark alley. He could not see Raul hiding in the shadows — only impenetrable darkness.

*What's this?* Thought Raul. *Has the mighty Sauriel lost his powers? Perhaps . . .*

"You're not really an angel, *Jack*. Are you? Simply a confused mortal."

Jack spun around to pinpoint Raul's voice, which seemed to come from all directions as it echoed off the alley walls.

Raul stalked Jack from behind. "Or, you did do it, *Sauriel*. You killed good ol' Ben Fuller. Because we both know: the side with the most souls wins."

Jack turned on his heels.

"A fallen angel. Now you and I will serve the same master. What a prize your soul will make. And, if it turns out you're not the angel, Sauriel, well, I'll enjoy killing Jack all the same." Raul threw the dagger.

Jack stepped aside and bolted down the alley. The dagger grazed his shoulder and penetrated deep into the wall behind him.

By the time Raul pried the dagger from the wall, Jack had rounded the corner, exited the alley, and into the path of Frank and Vijay.

"Bingo." Frank drew his gun on Jack.

Uniformed policemen emerged from Raul's building behind Jack. The only option would be to return to the alley, past Raul, and up a fire escape. Raul poked his head out of the shadows just far enough to meet Jack's gaze.

Jack raised his hands.

Mug Shot. Fingerprints. DNA Cheek Swab. Inside the Central Courthouse, Jack was booked on suspicion of murder for the deaths of Ben Fuller and at least two others. He would be held together with those arrested in the New York City borough of Manhattan and scheduled to appear before a judge. If he is ultimately convicted, or not released on bail, he would be transferred to jail or one of New York's upstate prisons.

In the courthouse lobby, Raul browsed the building directory.

*Central Booking, Records 141B. Third floor.*

Outside the courthouse, Raul scanned across the building's bulky façade of rust-colored concrete. The third-floor windows were narrow horizontal slits in the concrete, recessed and covered with metal bars. Raul spotted a cracked window and disappeared.

Inside the courthouse records room, Raul browsed through a basket of file records, "To Be Processed," and located a file that read "People v Wryder." He removed some of the papers from Jack's file, swapped them with documents from a different file, and snapped pictures of the new papers with his phone. "Oh, Jack," Raul hissed through yellowed dog teeth, "this will make you very unpopular."

Three unsavory convicts hunched over a bunk in their prison cell and played cards. The blanket vibrated and the cons exchanged a furtive glance as one of them withdrew a phone from beneath the mattress. Jack's mug shot and photos from a courthouse file appeared on the phone with the message: "On his way."

The con typed, "Do I know you?"

The reply was instant.

"Mutual friends in low places."

<hr />

The courthouse clerk was swamped by visitors and oblivious to the incessant ring of the desk phone. Frank approached the clerk and flashed his badge. "Detective Kelly, one-oh-one, eight."

The desk clerk scanned his computer screen. "Not listed."

"There has to be. There's an arraignment scheduled for my suspect. Check again. The whole schedule."

"Yep. One for Kelly. Suspect name: Jack S. Wryder."

"That's the one. I'm gonna be late."

"Really late. Mr. Wryder was transferred out two hours ago."

"Transferred? That's not possible. Where is he now?"

# Six

THE BUS ARRIVED at the prison receiving area and lurched to a stop. Hands and feet in heavy shackles, Jack shuffled down the steps of the bus. He bore the unfamiliar weight poorly, and his front foot missed the last step. Unable to raise his bound hands, it was his face that first reached the pavement. The reception guard shook his head at the unapologetic bus guards, who knew better than to let a shackled prisoner descend the steps alone.

Once the restraints were removed, the new arrivals were escorted through an enormous multilevel building of battleship-gray concrete and steel. Each level of the cavernous structure was comprised of hundreds of cells, which teemed with two thousand prisoners — many of whom leaned on railings with vacant stares down into the open common area.

Jack passed beneath the watchful eyes of several guards, who patrolled a narrow second-floor catwalk spanning the vast diameter of the building. The catwalk comprised a suspended metal walkway below which hung a row of industrial bay lights. His escorts paused to speak with a fellow guard, and Jack wandered away to observe the other prisoners. Racially self-segregated in gangs, some inmates sat around smooth-edged tables and played cards, some watched a large flat screen TV suspended from the wall, and others glared at the fresh fish paraded by the guards.

A small, mixed crowd of convicts from the various gangs coalesced around Jack. One of the convicts, a weaselly figure of a man with neo-Nazi tattoos, slithered through the crowd and shoved Jack from behind with a, "Hail Chomo," and pointing to the TV screen, he waved his hands and mocked, "*Angel of death*. Ooooo." The diverse crowd was fleetingly united in laughter. A few of the convicts spit on Jack.

Jack squared off for a fight, and a guard struck him on the head with a baton. Jack fell a second time. The guards half-carried, half-dragged Jack to his cell and shoved him inside. Jacks' cellmate recoiled. "You stay away from me," he whined, "I don't want nothin' to do with a *chomo*."

"Easy buddy," said Jack, feeling the bump swell on his head. "I'm not going to hurt you."

"Not worried about you, man." He pointed outside the cell. "It's them."

Three pairs of tattooed arms with bulging biceps flexed against the bars in an animalistic threat display. These were the same unsavory convicts that had received the courthouse file information that was switched by Raul.

"Last celly of a guy with short-eyes got burned. I mean charred, and not in a good way. They lit him up, and both 'em died in the fire. I'm not going down with you, man. We know what you are."

Jack stepped in close to his cell mate. "Really? What am I?"

"A chomo. Short-eyes. You . . . you raped that kid."
Jack stood dumbstruck.

---

*Jack tread lightly through the prison's common area and is recognized by a prisoner, an old man who calls out to him.*

*"Jack," says Ben Fuller. "You must do your part to receive His mercy. Once YOU are called by an angel of death, the time for mercy will be over — then you will meet only JUSTICE."*

*The prisoners above pound against their cell bars. They stretch their arms down toward Jack. A vacuous silence follows. It feels like every atom and molecule of air is being sucked out of the building.*

*"Sauriel. Sauriel," a demonic voice pierces the silence. "Will Sauriel come out and play?" Twisted, clawed hands spring from the floor to grab at Jack.*

*"Come. Join the party, Sauriel."*

*Disfigured demons with melted animal heads and reptilian limbs drip from the ceiling pipes and ooze up from cracks in the concrete floor. Sharp claws emerge to scratch and tear Jack's skin.*

*Raul appears before Jack, a severed ram's head dangling from his right hand, the ornamented dagger held in his left. "Won't be long now, Jack. It's time to accept your new master."*

"Wryder! Wryder!" the block officer shouted at Jack writhing on his cot.

Jack awoke disoriented from the parasomnia. His head ached terribly, whether from the blow of the guard's baton or wounds suffered in the demonic dream, Jack couldn't tell the difference.

"Gather your shit," the block officer continued. "You got a visitor."

The warden scrutinized the court order handed him by Frank. Frank leaned forward on the warden's desk. "Yeah. Big freakin' mistake. Wryder is to be remanded to my custody, effective immediately."

The block officer escorted Jack past the cells of the convicts who had marked him earlier. "They oughta give these guys the needle," quipped the officer.

"With death, any chance of redemption is lost," said Jack, reflecting on the fate of his own soul as much as the inmates who wanted to burn him alive.

"Get their evil asses outta here," growled the officer. "Not *my* problem."

Jack imagined the unredeemed souls of the convicts reanimated as demon warriors added to the ranks of the Forces of Darkness. That guy alone, Jack considered the largest of the convicts, he could take out a dozen guardians himself.

"Where these guys might go," said Jack, "becomes *everyone's* problem."

The block officer steered Jack along the second level walkway. Below in the common area, trouble brewed. Two dozen of the meanest-looking men, representing three different rival gangs, advanced towards each other.

Swastika, iron cross, and skinhead warrior's rune marked his face; an Aryan brother scraped a shiv across tabletops as he led the Brotherhood in a march along the edge of tables and chairs surrounding the common area.

Placaso tattoo across his beefy chest, penciled mustache and volcano goatee; the Mexican mafioso swaggered through and set up his gang beneath the large, flat screen TV.

Inked with the Big Gorilla Family's crossed machete and rifle, BGF con and his crew strutted in.

The cells were locked down. Guards filed in past Jack to fill the walkways and catwalk above the gathering storm. The block officer placed an arm across Jack's chest. "We hold here. We're not gonna make it to the Warden's office or back to your cell."

The phone buzzed and the Warden answered, "Yeah." He handed documents back to Frank and shook his head. "Are the crash gates closed?"

Frank overheard desperate shouts from the phone receiver. The Warden shouted uncomfortably back, "Meet at CP One and break the seals." To Frank, "You'll have to wait. We're in lock down."

BGF con slowly grasped and tugged at the back of a chair as if to politely offer a seat, and then he hurled it at the Mexican mafia. The chair *smashed* the TV screen and a shower of sparks rained on the mafia. The Mexicans charged. Aryan brother halted his gang with a fisted salute.

Above the melee, Jack was hemmed in by guards at one end of the catwalk. Toilet paper streamed down from the two thousand prisoners cheering the fight from above. The whole building had transformed into a steel colosseum. The BGF and Mexican gangs fought as junkyard gladiators wielding weapons of nail-studded broom handles, sharpened spoons, and chiseled toothbrushes.

The Aryan Brotherhood had held back like horses in a

starting gate, pressing and jittering at the edge of the fight. Once the Aryan brother was satisfied that the two rival gangs were fully engaged in close quarters combat, he opened his fist into a Nazi salute — a signal to his brothers to ignite and throw Molotov cocktails fashioned from cooking and motor oils, solvents, and naphthalene moth balls pilfered from the various prison workshops. A hail of rubber bullets fired by the guards upon the Aryans stopped the launch of all but one of the crude incendiary bottles. The bottle burst upon the concrete floor and fire billowed to within inches of the battling convicts.

Intense heat from the combustion and rapid spread of flames triggered the fire alarm and sprinkler system. The common area began to flood as the prison's lowest-bid drainage system was overwhelmed. Then the Aryans joined the melee.

Weary from the fight and maneuvering on a slippery surface awash with blood, sweat, and spreading flames, the Big Gorilla Family and Mexican gangs would have been easy prey to the fresh and eager Aryans. But before they could press their advantage, the flames swept across the surface of the water in waves that corralled *all* of the battling convicts together into a narrow area beneath the catwalk.

Forced to abandon the rumble by fire and an oily, choking smoke, the inmates scrambled onto chairs and hopped from table to table to escape the advancing flames. The fire swept on and engulfed the tables beneath their feet, squeezing them between walls of fire and into a ragged line beneath the catwalk.

To escape the flames, the inmates stacked chairs atop the

tables and jumped to grasp the catwalk cables that suspended the bay lights. The catwalk began to seesaw lengthwise under the weight of the inmates hanging from the lights. The guards had to hug the railings to keep from sliding off and into the flaming pit below. The catwalk tipped further, and one of the guards spilled over the railing. He held on for his life.

"Cut the damn cable! Cut it! Or we all go over!" cried the guard who desperately clung to the catwalk railing.

The catwalk had rotated nearly vertical, the guards held fast, and the inmates dangled above the flooded floor. One of the guards left Jack's side to unlock a fire axe and hacked away at the metal cables suspending the catwalk.

*Snap-Twang!* The catwalk righted itself with a violent jolt then teetered and bobbed like a ginormous canoe above waves of dying flame. The combustible fuel from the Molotov cocktail was spent. A brief, collective sigh of relief erupted from the guards that began to make their way off the catwalk and onto the more secure walkways.

The inmates began to look for a safe way down from the bay light cables from which they remained suspended. As they shimmied along the cables hand-over-hand toward the walkways at the ends of the catwalk, a grating, metallic noise seized everyone's attention. Somewhere, a large metal cable was snaking loose.

The row of bay lights, to which the convicts desperately clung, unzipped from below the catwalk, and together the row of heavy lights and inmates plunged to the flooded floor. One by one, the lamps hit the floor and exploded in showers of hot sparks and pops.

The inmates, many of whom still grasped the suspension

cable, were paralyzed on the flooded ground into a macabre "mannequin challenge" as high voltage coursed through their wet bodies. Above them, impassive guards held their safe positions along the walkways.

The inmates above, who a moment before had cheered the violent clash from their cells, rattled the bars and shouted down at the guards to save their fellow inmates. The guards slammed batons against the bars and failing to deter their screams began to strike their hands.

Jack watched the convicts below. Their jaws clenched and limbs trembled as the electrical current surged through their bodies.

There was an electrical cabinet and a large, red-handled safety switch at the opposite end of the catwalk. A gnarled-face guard followed Jack's gaze to the cabinet, stepped in front of it, and smirked. Jack turned to his block officer and pleaded, "You must do something. Cut the power."

The block officer hesitated. Jack grabbed at the officer's radio and was struck hard from behind by another guard. Jack fell a third time. On his knees, Jack watched the dying cons — among them were familiar faces from the crowd that had mocked and spat on him when he first arrived at the prison. Jack rose to his feet and faced down a gauntlet of guards between him and the catwalk.

Jack punched and kicked his way through the throng of guards. There were just too many bodies in his way, and he was stopped just short of the catwalk. Jack had no sooner thought that he had failed when the guards parted before him and opened a clear path to the electrical switch. Jack stepped into the breach.

His block officer reached out and yanked Jack by the shirt as the gnarled-faced guard stepped in front of the switch, leveled a shotgun at Jack's chest, and pulled the trigger. The blast missed Jack and struck the block officer square in the trauma plate of his ballistic vest.

Jack tore out of his shirt, rolled over the catwalk railing, and dropped hard on his back atop a charred table. The impact of the fall and searing heat of the table's surface blazed up his spine. The worst of his pain was mitigated by an adrenaline rush that was boosted further by the sight of another electrical cabinet and safety switch located in the common area. Jack struggled to his feet atop the table. The electrical cabinet was located against the far wall. To avoid the electrified floor, he had to step from rickety, fire-torn table to table across the common area, which he managed to traverse to within several feet of the switch. Jack could smell the burnt hair and skin of the convicts frying toward death by electrocution. Jack inhaled and stepped to the floor.

A *shockwave* of electrical current surged through Jack's body, sweeping through the deep tissues of his muscles, nerves, and organs. The high voltage heated Jack from inside out. He knew he had only seconds to summon the will and muster the strength to overcome his increasing loss of voluntary muscle control. It was an agonizing shuffle toward the switch. Jack fought for every breath as the electrical current contracted every muscle in the walls of his chest.

He neared the switch. Sparks burned his skin. He had exhausted his strength. Gone was the hormone rush that had helped carry him this far. Unable to control his arms and fingers, Jack leaned clumsily for the switch and hooked his trembling hand over the handle. Respiratory arrest and ventricular fibrillation did the rest of the work. Jack lost consciousness and fell backward, pulling the switch.

Frank followed the stretcher outside and joined the EMTs in the back of the ambulance. Jack was unconscious, and his head was dressed in blood-soaked bandages where his skull had met the concrete floor.

The hours waiting in the intensive care unit were unbearable, more so after Frank had drained the coffee machine dry. His prime suspect in the hospital murders might be dead before he had answers to any of a dozen questions. When the doctor finally arrived with an update, Frank's caffeinated jump from his seat scattered a dozen paper cups to the floor.

"His breathing and heart rhythm are now stable," reported the doctor. "However, he sustained a traumatic head injury and remains unresponsive."

Frank nodded, and the doctor continued with a puzzled look on her face. "Has Dr. Wryder been diagnosed or treated for mental illness, sleep disorders, or dissociative identity disorder?" To which Frank shrugged.

"How well do you know him?" The doctor leafed through Jack's patient file. "Any indication he suffered from hallucinations or delusions? Believes he has a grand purpose, or special powers?"

Frank cocked his head. "I don't follow, doc."

"His reticular activating system," the Doctor showed Frank an image of Jack's brain in the file, "the nerve pathways in his brainstem, here, show extensive lesions."

"From the shock and fall," Frank reasoned.

"No, Sir. In treating the obvious injury, we discovered unrelated, pre-existing neurological disease. Dr. Wryder's brain was damaged long before his fall."

The prospect of an insanity plea from pre-existing brain damage was unwelcome news to Frank. He leaned heavily on the counter of the ICU nurses' station and considered how this new wrinkle in the case would affect his investigation. Several people at Memorial Hospital, this hospital, had died under circumstances that could not be explained by the patients' health condition or current medical treatment. The one piece of tangible evidence that connected each of the deaths was some sort of odd pattern in the patients' heart monitor at the time of death. EKG tracings, or was it ECG? Whatever the nurses and doctors saw, it didn't make sense to them. Frank's investigation and background checks revealed that all but one of the patients, Ben Fuller, had committed horrible acts — criminal or otherwise. Now we add Dr. Jack Wryder to the mix. Wryder was seen leaving the scene of Ben Fuller's death, and he was in the room at the time of another patient's death. Then he ran. Why did Wryder run? His job was in the hospital morgue, not with live patients. But by all accounts, Wryder spent *all* of his breaks and afterwork hours visiting patients. That certainly would provide him with the opportunity to get to know the patients well enough to judge them. Plus, there were the missing patient records that could have provided Wryder with the information on whether the patient was expected to die without his intervention. If we ignore Ben Fuller's death, thought Frank, or assume there was something awful about Fuller that Wryder knew and others didn't, then perhaps we have a clear motive. A sick, twisted motive. But nothing new.

Frank recalled the case of hospital nurse, Charles Edmund Cullen. Cullen was an American serial killer who in 2003 confessed to the murder of over twenty of his patients. Frank was familiar with the case, which took place right across the river in New Jersey. And there have been over a dozen other so called, "angel of death," or angel of mercy, hospital killers. A common thread in the psyche of these killers was the sense of control the killers felt. For some it included a sense of duty or purpose, such as relieving the pain and suffering of the patients. Or a belief that it was their responsibility, a special calling, to kill a patient. In some way, these killers believed the world would be better if the person was dead.

"Believes he has a grand purpose, or special powers?" That is what the doctor had asked him about Wryder. That would fit, reasoned Frank. Jack killed patients that he believed needed to die. A diseased brain might also explain Jack's strung-out appearance when he and Vijay first met Wryder at his apartment. Wryder looked like he hadn't slept in days. There was the empty pill bottle visible on the floor of his apartment and the account from one of Wryder's colleagues, Kevin what's-his-name. Frank took out his notepad and leafed through it. Yeah, here it is. "Observed Jack sneaking pills from a bottle in his lab coat. Headaches. Massaged temples."

Whether or not Jack had "hallucinations or delusions," Frank predicted that when Wryder was interrogated, no doubt with a high-priced lawyer present, there would be all sorts of "the neighbor's dog told me to do it" testimony. Wryder's preexisting brain damage would make this case a slam dunk for the "angel of death" legal defense team. Frank wouldn't even need to follow up on the missing patients' records . . . Records Room. The sign on the wall caught Frank's attention. "Someone noticed that some charts for patients were missing. That's what got people's attention in the first place." Frank had said as much to Vijay when he was first asked about the murders. "Otherwise, nobody would've noticed." Frank followed the signs to the Records Room.

The Department of Forensic Biology in New York City's Office of Chief Medical Examiner (OCME) runs the largest public DNA crime laboratory in the world. The OCME employs over one-hundred and fifty forensic DNA scientists conducting blood and DNA testing on at least 40,000 items of evidence every year. That year's item #9971 was the DNA sample taken from Jack Sauriel Wryder, a suspected serial killer. The Angel of Death.

Forensic evidence from the suspicious deaths at Memorial Hospital was lacking. Autopsy results for the hospital victims had ruled out death from preexisting illness or current medical treatment including faulty ventilation equipment, though the forensic pathologists concluded that the victims were most likely smothered or suffocated. But there were no identifiable signs of forced asphyxiation, such as the tiny hemorrhages, or petechiae, that form as small veins are broken by high pressure in the blood vessels of the eyes and skin. None of the victims had bloodshot eyes or bruises. Without any direct forensic evidence, the circumstantial evidence would need to be overwhelming to prove murder in this high-profile case. DNA samples collected from hospital workers and DNA found in hair follicles and shafts collected from crime scene pillow covers, bed linens, blankets, etc. might at least place a murder suspect in the room of each of the suspicious deaths.

A young forensic technician threw back an energy shot and entered the password to start up the integrated criminal DNA database application for the hundred and fifty-third time that week. And for the hundred and fifty-third time he waited for completion of the frustratingly slow splash screen of the Ladonscorp Industries logo — a dark-green, five-pointed star. "Screw the security protocols. This takes way too long to launch. I'm tempted to stay logged in. What's the file ID for the Wryder sequence?"

"Remember? It's the same as the sample item number," replied the salt-and-pepper-haired senior tech.

"Right. Forgot. Thanks. Got 'em." The young tech tapped in the sample item number and ran the search against the databases that contained tens of millions of DNA profiles. "No matches in UCODIS," replied the young tech as the results scrolled on the screen.

Zero Matches: Universal Combined DNA Index System.

The screen went blank.

An error message flashed on the screen accompanied by harsh *beeps*.

ERROR. Contact Deinogen.

The young tech banged on the keypad. "Systems locked up."

"Don't bang on it, numbskull. What the hell did you do?"

"Nothing. It says to contact the database company."

The senior tech crowded in to look at the screen. "Never saw that before."

"Should I reboot? Run the sequence again?"

"Yeah. It's worth a shot. In any case, we need to get the system back online, or today's testing schedule will get all jammed up."

"You need to see this." Frank stormed into the office and held his phone in front of the captain's face. "I thought, maybe we could show that Wryder's actions were premeditated. You know, involved the careful plannin' and execution of a *sound* mind."

The captain squinted at the phone screen for a few seconds. "What am I looking at, Frank?"

"Watch. After patient charts were discovered missin', the hospital installed a camera inside the records room. But they were only lookin' for people who shouldn't have access."

On screen was an overhead shot of an orderly browsing through rows of files. The orderly selects one folder, and then he exits the room.

"And?" asked the captain.

Frank rewound the video, played it, and paused it. "Here. As the orderly passes below the camera on the way out of the room, he tucks the patient's record inside his shirt. Why hide the file?" Before the captain could respond. "He wasn't carryin' anythin' else. His hands were free."

"Frank —"

"Captain, the guy in the video is Raul Noma. The one connected to Jack Wryder."

# Seven

*". . . ships magnetic shield, like that of the Earth's, was intended to protect Colonel Iverson from the powerful galactic cosmic radiation that has plagued previous long range space missions. A special commission has been formed to investigate the tragic accident, which occurred . . ."*

THE HARSH LIGHTS OF THE TELEVISION snapped off, replaced by the soft glow of moonlight through the hospital room window.

The young nurse placed the remote beside the bed where Jack lay unconscious, one of his hands cuffed to the bed. Under the watchful eye of a uniformed policeman, she checked the heart monitor — the soft beeps of a normal heart rhythm — and traced the electrodes back to Jack's chest. She felt for bends or kinks along the i.v. connections that led from the insertion site in the arm — no signs and symptoms of phlebitis or infection, normal skin temperature — up to the solution bag hanging from the pole. After verifying the infusion rate, she noted the amount of solution remaining in the bag and left the room followed by her police escort.

The privacy curtain rippled in a breeze that slipped through a crack in the window.

Raul appeared beside Jack.

Frank marched through the hospital lobby and up to the reception desk. "Jack Wryder's room." The receptionist handed him a pass. Frank's phone buzzed.

"Find anythin'?" he answered.

Vijay and crime scene investigators were inside Raul's apartment. The place was tossed upside down.

"Bingo, Frank."

Vijay surveyed a pile of items that had been found beneath a pried-up floorboard. Among the items were news clippings about people accused or convicted of human trafficking, rape, and murder. There were patient charts from Memorial Hospital with highlighted text: "prognosis is good", "expected to recover", and "in remission." And there were photographs. Lots of photographs. Images of patients asleep in their hospital beds. Vijay recognized a few of the patients as known victims. There was at least a dozen more.

*Flash.*

Raul put the photo in his pocket and tucked the instant camera beneath his uniform.

He covered Jack's nose and mouth with his hands and grinned expectantly at the heart monitor.

Nothing.

*Normal heart rhythm, no flatline.* Raul's crooked smile turned to a scowl. "How —" Raul choked as the metal cross bar from the i.v. pole was jammed up against his throat.

Jack sat forward. "See you on the other side." And thrusting the pole, forced Raul back against the wall. Raul kicked and thrashed about. The base of the i.v. stand detached from the pole and sailed across the room. The clatter of the struggle did not go unnoticed.

The policeman rushed into the room to investigate. Raul, smartly dressed in hospital whites, was violently pinned to the wall by the prisoner and murder suspect. It was obvious who was the victim. The policeman wrest the pole from Jack's hand and freed Raul, who promptly attacked the policeman from behind with a chokehold. Jack lunged forward, restrained and struggling against the handcuffs. The policeman collapsed at the foot of the bed. Raul turned his attention back to Jack.

Jack tore the electrodes off his chest.

The moment Frank stepped off the elevator, the heart monitor alarm *blared* at the nurse's station. "Code Blue, seventy-three, twenty-six," the duty nurse shouted. Frank joined the nurse in a race into Jack's room.

Open handcuffs dangled from the empty bed. The policeman was slumped on the floor, unconscious but alive, and pantless.

Gideon's bulk filled the doorway to the shelter. His eyes followed the unlikely duo of detectives back to their unmarked car.

"John Smith?" Vijay asked Frank, "Why John Smith?"

"Wryder gave them an alias. A common name."

"Oh," Vijay nodded, "An Ashok Kumar."

"An Ashush?" Frank shook his head to clear his muddled thoughts. "Whatever. Wryder used a homeless shelter. That means he's desperate and on his own. But the connection with Raul Noma. That bugs me." Frank tapped out his thoughts on the steering wheel. "Wryder might have been lookin' for what ya' found in Noma's apartment. Evidence of the murders."

"Then why not explain that to the police? Why is Wryder running from us?"

"Noma's guilt wouldn't make Wryder innocent. He was placed at the scene of two deaths. That would explain Wryder's fear of the police. And the evidence in Raul's apartment coulda' been planted."

"Yes. But we only searched Noma's place *after* you saw the records room video. A coincidence, Frank?"

"Wryder could've put the evidence in Noma's apartment. Or, Wryder was being blackmailed by Noma. Or . . ."

"Both Wryder and Noma are working together," exclaimed Vijay, pointing a proud finger in the air.

Frank wrung the life out of the steering wheel. "Then why would Wryder pretend to be Noma's brother to get the address to his apartment? Other than the fingerprints, you found nothin' in Noma's apartment that explains a connection to Wryder?"

"Nothing, Frank."

"What did forensics say about what ya' found in the fridge?"

"Nothing out of the ordinary, Frank. Just an uncooked ham, a nine-pound, salt-cured ham on a plate. Not kosher."

"And not helpful." Frank yanked the car into gear, and they pulled away from the shelter.

Skulking in the rooftop shadows, two men spoke in low voices.

"Hey man," said Smoker. "I told you what I told the cops. Now where's the stuff? You said it would give me a super high."

"Oh yes," replied Raul. "Here is your high . . ." Raul plunged his ornamented dagger into Smoker's belly and lifted him off the roof, ". . . now here is your low." Raul heaved Smoker over the edge of the rooftop.

"' . . . and falling headlong, he burst open in the middle and all his entrails gushed out." Raul savored the impact of Smoker's body onto the pavement.

"Give my regards to Judas."

Gideon rose from his chair with a glance at the moon outside the window, as if the moon had foretold Jack's return.

"Ms. Ward would like to see you." Gideon nodded toward the office door behind him.

"Sure," said Jack, "but first I need to use the —"

"Now," insisted Gideon. "You will see Ms. Ward, now."

Jack sized up the giant Gideon. He squeezed past Gideon and into the office.

Sarah was busy at her desk shuffling papers. She spoke without looking up.

"Tell me, Jack, do I strike you as someone who harbors criminals?"

"Listen," Jack replied.

Sarah slapped the top of the desk. "No. You listen. The police asked me to contact them if you returned. I don't care if people come to us, ashamed, use fake names. But I have no tolerance for people that use me, use this shelter, to hide from —"

"I'm not a criminal. And I have no intention of using you or anyone else. I'll leave now and cause no trouble." Jack turned to leave.

"Jack. Come back and sit down."

Jack hesitated.

"Sit down, Jack. Nobody's going to call the police."

"Why should I trust you? Why would you want to help me?"

"I can see you're troubled. You're confused and desperate, but I don't believe you're a murderer."

Jack settled into the chair.

"What's your story, Jack?"

"You wouldn't believe me."

"Trust me, Jack. You might be surprised."

Jack gazed into Sarah's ameliorative eyes. "I'm not Jack Wryder," he spilled. "Well, I wasn't always."

# Eight

EXPRESSIONLESS, SARAH CONSIDERED JACK for a while before she broke the silence.

"So, you're going for an insanity plea."

"I knew you wouldn't believe me. I'm even beginning to doubt myself. Give me enough time to sort things out and a place to stay while I take care of a few things."

"Jack, the police can return here at any time. I can't risk the city shutting down this shelter. You can't stay here indefinitely."

"I know. I'll find another place."

"Where will you go?"

"I don't know."

Sarah searched Jack's eyes. "We . . . I have a friend. First thing tomorrow, I'll take you to him. Maybe we can get you that time you need to "sort things out." I'll have Gideon set up a cot here in my office for tonight. And . . ." Sarah smirked at Jack, his hospital gown was tucked inside baggy policeman's pants, ". . . see if we can find you clothes that fit."

Gideon escorted Jack out of the office, and Sarah leaned back in her chair.

*Assigned to release the souls of the dead. Right here in New York City.*

Sarah had listened patiently, as Jack had explained, rather matter-of-factly, that he is one of many beings sent from a place in the multiverse — an infinite number of parallel universes — and assigned to planet Earth to release the souls of the dead. Jack made a point to clarify that only a small percentage of human souls get directly released by his kind. Most human souls depart on their own after death and await "processing" in an intermediate location, or as some humans call it, purgatory. Most "facilitated releases," the type that Jack performed, are only authorized to provide a representative sample to monitor trends in the overall state of humanity. Under no circumstance, ever, was a soul permitted to be released before its time. And that's where Jack's troubles began.

According to Jack, who appears to have been bored with his assignment on Earth, souls were being released at the hospital without permission. And to make matters worse, these "unauthorized releases" were the souls of truly wicked people that would go to a place in the multiverse where they would become warriors in the "forces of darkness."

"Sarah, as we sit here, battles rage across the heavens. I intended to release more people with good souls to help in the war against evil. Ben Fuller had a pure soul, and he was expected to die anyway. And the pain." Jack had paused, and Sarah had sensed the conflict within him. "I just can't recall that night in the hospital."

Because of Ben Fuller's death, Jack had explained, his own soul is now destined to serve the forces of darkness unless he restores a hundred souls to good before he dies. He believes that at least one "demon" is working to make his death happen sooner than later.

Jack also claims that this same demon possesses an orderly, who is murdering patients at the hospital. He just can't prove it *yet*.

Of course, thought Sarah, it was just her luck that Jack Sauriel Wryder had picked her homeless shelter as a hideout. She could only imagine what other troubles the releaser had brought to her door.

Across from the shelter, a streetlamp cast long, misty shadows on damp pavement. Out of the shadows, Raul emerged.

Sarah returned for Jack in the morning, and they left the shelter together, strolling shoulder to shoulder past a horse and carriage. Sarah brushed Jack's arm. "My friend's place is not far from the park."

All the previous days' dampness had evaporated into a light mist that swirled up from around their feet. Jack inhaled the pleasantly incongruent odors of fresh baked bread, cut grass, motor oil, and horse manure. "All the time I've been down here, I've never been to Central Park."

"It is a beautiful place," said Sarah. "How long have you lived in the city?"

"It feels like an eternity."

A horse snorted, and Jack turned. A dark figure ducked behind the carriage. The horse, unnerved by the hidden figure, repeated the alarm. Jack grasped Sarah's arm, and they quickened their pace.

"Maybe this wasn't such a good idea," said Jack.

Sarah mistook a passing police car as Jack's concern. "Don't worry, Jack, it's not much further. Just a few more blocks past the —"

Jack pushed Sarah into an open cab, pulled the door shut behind them, and locked it.

"Jack?" Sarah retreated from him, annoyed and confused.

"Go!" Jack yelled to the cab driver.

The driver glanced at Jack in the rearview mirror. "Okay buddy, where to?"

Raul slammed himself against the locked door and pressed his face hard against the window glass.

"Just go!"

The cab pulled away from the curb. Jack and Sarah looked back. The distance widened between the car and Raul.

"Jack, do you know him?"

*That window is open!* Jack reached over Sarah to press the window button. "Keep it closed, Sarah. It can use the space to get inside." Jack felt around the edges of the other windows to ensure they were completely sealed.

"Jack, tell me what's going on?"

"That was the real murderer."

Sarah looked back and watched Raul pick up his pace from a walk to a jog to a run and was gaining on them quickly.

The cab stopped short, and the cabbie spoke over his shoulder. "The President's in town. Backs up everything."

Jack spied a horse and four-wheeled carriage on the park side of the road. The carriage driver was off on the sidewalk, preoccupied haggling a fare.

"Get out," Jack said to Sarah, and they sprang from the cab.

Jack ushered Sarah onto the carriage, and he gripped the reins.

"You know how to handle a horse?" asked Sarah.

"Comes with the job."

*Right. Grim reaper,* she thought.

Jack whistled and the carriage lurched forward.

"How we doing?" asked Jack.

The horse and carriage rapidly outpaced Raul. "He's falling back," replied Sarah. "But not for long."

The clobbered owner of a motor scooter lay sprawled on the sidewalk. Raul mounted the scooter.

Jack commanded the horse with a distinctive *whistle.* The horse kicked up its rear legs high with great force, and the carriage jolted forward. Jack veered the carriage off the street and into the park. Raul followed.

The carriage was designed for slow, romantic rides around the park. At high speed and in rough terrain, the carriage began to shake apart, leaving a trail of jingling bells and tack bouncing off behind it. Raul slowed and weaved to avoid the noisy debris, then accelerated off onto a path that ran parallel to the carriage.

The carriage continued to shed pieces as it bounced and rattled along. It wasn't clear which of the lost parts might be required to control the carriage and keep them from crashing. Raul erupted from the dense foliage alongside the carriage, and he reached for Sarah. She narrowly escaped his grasp as Jack swerved the carriage away and then back toward Raul.

Raul swerved to avoid a lamp post. The carriage was not so maneuverable. One of the carriages four wooden wheels crashed into a fire hydrant and showered Jack with splinters. What was left of the carriage swerved wildly from left to right. Jack steered the crippled carriage into a narrow path designed for bikes and pedestrians.

Raul reappeared at their side, and swerving in unison with the carriage, he grabbed for the carriage's long hand brake. Jack and Sarah moved to deflect him. Too late.

The carriage *squealed, cracked*, and skid to a halt. Jack tightened his grip on the reins and was thrown from the carriage. His body snapped back hard between the horse and carriage.

Raul overshot the carriage. He spun the scooter around, kicking up a cloud of dirt, and charged.

Dazed from the collision, Jack shook off the pain and found Sarah lying in the wrecked carriage. She appeared unconscious. Jack took her pulse. "You'll be fine," he muttered, reasoning that Sarah's good soul would be of no use to Raul.

Raul bore down on Jack.

Jack mounted the horse, unfastened what little remained of the connection between horse and carriage, ripped off the horse's blinders, and *whistled*. The horse, free of the wrecked carriage, kicked up its rear legs with a *whinny* and took off with fresh vigor, maneuvering out of Raul's path and over a low fence. Raul charged past the wreck and crashed into the fence.

Sarah opened her eyes, and with an enigmatic smile, watched Jack gallop away.

A motorcycle cop arrived to check on Raul.

Blood gushed down Raul's forehead and stung his eyes. The scooter was scattered about him in pieces.

"You all right?" asked the cop.

Raul grinned maniacally at his good fortune.

"I'll call for an amb—"

Raul brained the policeman unconscious with the handlebars of the scooter. The force of the blow knocked off the cop's helmet. Raul squeezed his own bleeding head into the helmet, blood and sweat dripped down his face and neck.

With neither sight nor sound of Raul, Jack slowed down to rest just inside the shade of an overpass. The horse lowered its head, and its chest heaved with labored breaths. Jack dismounted and noticed the horse's legs were studded with splintered wood. He gave the animal a kind pat. "And you still ran like the devil himself was chasing us."

A motorcycle *growled* in the distance. Covered from head to tailpipe in blood and sweat, Raul looked the motorcycle cop from hell.

Jack hoist himself back on the horse. "I'm going to need a little more of your help." Deeper within the overpass, Jack noticed a door propped open with an orange construction cone.

Jack rode the horse slowly through a clean, well-lit maintenance tunnel. Strings of incandescent light bulbs dangled from the painted walls. The *clip-clop* of the horse's hooves echoed throughout the tunnel. In an adjacent passage, men in hard hats ate their lunch.

"You hear that?" asked one of the workmen.

"Yeah, and I heard stories," said another. "Rats the size of small dogs."

Raul circled back through the park and sped beneath the overpass. He missed the maintenance tunnel door. Jack had removed the construction cone and closed the door.

Jack entered a maze of incomplete tunnels. Few bulbs lit the moldy, concrete passages. The deeper he rode, the darker it became. The ground softened as well, and the horse's hooves bit into the gravel floor, leaving a trail of horseshoe prints. "Show me the way," Jack whispered, "'. . . and make the crooked places straight.'"

Raul's eyes darted back and forth between the paths ahead and the overpass where he had last seen Jack. He paused, revved up the motorcycle, spun the bike around, and sped back to the overpass.

Jack navigated toward the sound of trains in the distance. He crouched low on the horse to avoid the many hanging pipes and wires. Among the sounds of the trains, emerged the distant *growl* of a motorcycle. Jack paused in the tunnel, which was bathed in the dim red hue of emergency lights.

*Roaring* through the tunnels, Raul followed the horse's hoof prints.

Jack raced off, ducking to avoid decapitation by the pipes and loose wires. A light shone at the end of the tunnel. The conditions in the tunnel improved, and the horse's hooves found solid ground. Ahead, the tunnel would open into a large area of underground train platforms. This was the lower level of Grand Central Terminal, where crowds of commuters and other travelers departed from trains onto platforms. From there, they would file toward the lower-level entrance to the terminal.

Seated low on the motorcycle, Raul easily avoided the overhead obstacles and closed in on Jack. The front fender of the motorcycle *dinged* and *sparked* against the rear shoes of the horse.

As Raul crouched down for the final, fatal assault, he glimpsed a low wall directly ahead. The side of a raised platform cut across their path. Raul slid to a stop. But Jack appeared certain to crash into the wall.

Atop the train platform, the echo of approaching *hoofbeats* elicited confused looks from bewildered commuters. From below the platform, a horse bolted out of the dark, landed atop the platform, and clacked and skidded to a stop. Jack looked upon the astonished crowd.

"Hi-ho Silver?"

Down inside the access tunnel, Raul pulled up to an emergency phone box.

The transit officer assigned to the Metro North Police desk had a clear view inside the busy lower terminal. He listened briefly to the caller on the emergency line and grumbled to his colleague, "Some joker on box phone six says there's a terrorist in the tunnel, on a horse. Send someone down to check it out." As he reached to hang up the phone, he saw Jack emerge inside the lower terminal.

Jack slowly worked his way on horseback through the crowd. Entangled with frayed harness lines and debris picked up in the tunnel, the horse's saddle bag resembled an improvised explosive device.

"A bomb," the officer shouted. "We got a guy on a horse in the terminal and a possible IED."

Marble wall tiles *exploded* next to Jack's head. Jack had made his way along the ramp that led to the upper-level of the terminal when a national guardsman unloaded his M4 carbine at him.

The gunfire triggered panic. People screamed and fled in all different directions. Jack escaped up the ramp and passed a bewildered little girl who had become separated from her parents. The crowd stampeded toward her.

Jack returned through a hail of gunfire, scooped up the little girl, and together atop the horse they bolted up the ramp and out of the terminal onto 42nd Street, where Jack deposited her safely beside a taxi stand.


Inside the security command center, police technicians viewed digital images of Jack atop the horse. Using facial recognition software, they worked a close-up image.

Various faces cycled through on the screen before it froze on an image of Jack. "WANTED NYPD," read one of the techs. "We have a local match."

At each attempt at a bite, Frank flinched at the *bang* of the jackhammer and spilled his food. He and Vijay were parked outside an Indian restaurant located across from a construction site. Frank scooped up another bit of the curry with a piece of naan as Vijay munched away, oblivious to the noise and Frank's growing frustration.

"How the hell?" growled Frank. "I give up. I'm gettin' a dirty water dog."

The radio crackled, "Man on a horse, heading down 42nd Street toward the East River. Subject is identified as Jack Wryder. Wanted by NYPD in connection with several homicides. He is carrying an explosive device."

"Explosives?" Frank croaked through his first successful mouthful of food.

"On a horse?" added Vijay.

At the same moment, several blocks south of Frank and Vijay, Raul cruised down the street on the police motorcycle he had stolen in the park. ". . . identified as Jack Wryder. Wanted by NYPD in . . ." Raul accelerated down the street weaving through the traffic.

Jack slumped atop the sweaty horse, and together they plod quietly along the East River Promenade. Jack wondered where he would go from there. The homeless shelter would no longer be safe, and he had already put Sarah Ward in danger. He almost lost his own life. How could he ever hope to stay alive long enough to save the souls of others? It came down to him and this horse. And he would have to leave the horse — it was far too conspicuous.

Jack leaned to gaze over a low stone wall. It was a steep drop to rusty metal debris that spiked up from the river below.

Sudden *revving* of a motorcycle startled the horse, violently bucking Jack off his back. Jack landed hard atop the wall, aggravating the injuries from his fall in the prison.

Raul dismounted the motorcycle, drew the policeman's baton from the bike, and aimed to crush Jack's skull.

Jack grabbed a loose stone from the wall and launched it into the side of Raul's head. The force of the blow shattered the visor of the motorcycle helmet and knocked Raul to the ground.

Jack hopped off the wall, "No more running."

Raul started to rise, and Jack delivered several more crushing blows with the stone. Raul staggered to his feet. Jack swung hard and wide for the final knockout. Raul disappeared.

The momentum of the heavy stone in Jack's hand carried him off balance.

"Swing and a miss!" Raul reappeared behind Jack. "My turn," and he drove a home run swing of the police baton into Jack's back, sending Jack over the wall.

Jack dangled high above the river. He clung to the cliff wall by the pads of his fingertips curled over thin edges in the wall. His thumbs pressed on top of his index fingers to lock them in place. Jack struggled against the searing pain of his finger joints and tendons stretching to their limit.

Saliva-thickened blood bubbled down Raul's chin, and he hissed through a sardonic smile, "Time to meet your maker's monster."

Glancing down at the river below, Jack followed a bead of sweat drop from the tip of his nose and split upon the sharp edge of rusty metal. Raul raised the baton and delivered a bone shattering blow to Jack's left hand. Jack withdrew it and barely held on with the other. Raul grinned and raised the baton to deliver the final blow.

Jack *whistled.*

The horse *whinnied.*

Raul knit his brow. Then his jaw exploded with the impact of the rear hoof of the horse. Teeth and blood spout out of Raul's mouth, and his body collapsed on the wall.

Jack used Raul's body for leverage and pulled himself up.

"What a magnificent moonrise . . . sunset," thought Jack as he caught his breath and rolled Raul's body over the wall. "Never noticed."

Frank and Vijay stepped out of the car, guns drawn, and surveyed the scene: bloodied horse, bloodied police helmet, bloodied stones. Vijay leaned over the wall. Rusty metal littered a rusty river.

Frank holstered his weapon. "What the hell happened here?"

The horse stomped a hoof on bloodied teeth.

Deep inside the park, concealed in the moonlight shadow of a large boulder, Jack reclined and closed his eyes against hunger, exhaustion, pain, vulnerability. Jack contemplated his mortality. He found courage, exhilaration, satisfaction, and pleasure. He had no need for a grand purpose or special powers. Perhaps being human was . . .. His head ached, and he rubbed his temples. But there was the mission. He had figured out the *real* purpose of his assignment.

Beaming lights stirred Jack to his feet.

Gabriel emerged out of the headlights.

"Raul Noma was my real mission. Wasn't it, Gabriel? Uncover and identify the demon at the hospital and stop it."

Gabriel took Jack's arm and guided him out of the headlights and toward a limousine.

"We wanted to see if you were up to the task," said Gabriel.

"Up to the task?" Jack huffed. "Fine. Mission accomplished. Now *you* need to buy me more time to save the hundred and redeem my soul."

Gabriel opened the limo door. "You are right. You have not saved a hundred souls. You saved a thousand."

Jack paused mid-step.

*From each upper level of the Main Prison Block, across rows of hundreds of cells, two thousand inmates in silent awe witness Jack's agony and selfless rescue of the convicts.*

*Jack lies motionless, arms outstretched, blood and water flow around his head.*

*In the eyes of the prisoners and the guards who hang their heads in shame, even the hardest of hearts appear to soften.*

"In finding our weakness, we discover our strength," said Gabriel. He searched Jack's eyes. "You cannot remember anything from the night Ben Fuller died."

Jack shook his head.

"Because you were not meant to remember. Ben Fuller died a natural death. Though his death helped make a powerful point. We could not very well have one of our "angels" go rogue. Could we? Not with the battles we have raging elsewhere." Gabriel dug into his pocket, "And from what you have shown us . . ." Gabriel rattled an unlabeled bottle of pills. "We have bigger plans for you, Jack Wryder."

Gabriel tossed the bottle to Jack and then presented him with a manila envelope. On the cover of the envelope was a dark-green, five-pointed star, the Ladonscorp Industries logo, below which was boldly typed: "Project Osiris."

"Your full power will be restored. You are going to need it." Gabriel nodded toward the open door.

Jack ducked into the car, where someone else was already seated.

"Hello, Jack," Sarah said with a warm smile. "Welcome back."

"Sarah?"

Sarah revealed a glimpse of her angelic form.

"You never really were alone, Jack."

The limousine pulled away, up a wide avenue and into a supermoon. Jack caught the reflection of the driver in the rearview mirror. Gideon. He flashed Jack with an ear-to-ear grin.

Jack leaned forward and whispered in Gideon's ear, "Before anything else. I need to make one stop."


Nothing in this world, or any other, could have stopped Jack from keeping a pinky promise. He snuck into Emily's hospital room.

"Hey squirt." . . . Jack faltered.

Emily was unconscious and mechanically ventilated. She was receiving end-of-life care.

Jack stifled tears and put a stuffed toy lion beside Emily. Then he moved it. And again. No matter where he placed the lion, it felt wrong. *What would a dying girl care about this silly, little* . . . Jack squeezed the animal so hard he burst the seams.

He removed the ventilator from Emily's pallid face. She managed a few final, labored breaths and *flatlined*.

Jack cupped one hand and held it motionless, palm down, above Emily's forehead. Across his skin from fingertips to elbow, dark stripes appeared, and one by one, like passing clouds, the bands rippled across his skin.

Emily's face brightened.

Color returned to her cheeks.

"Jaaack," spoke a voice from above.

**END OF BOOK TWO**

## About The Author

JOHN ELGAN changed from a career in big pharma to teach science to high school and college students. He has used storytelling to activate his students' imagination, deep thinking, and emotions to help them make meaningful connections in life beyond the classroom. John is also the author of short stories, four of which are published in *Yellow Diamond: Cautionary Tales of Science Fiction & Fantasy.*

You can find book discussion questions and sign up for updates at johnelgan.com

www.ingramcontent.com/pod-product-compliance
Lightning Source LLC
Chambersburg PA
CBHW030540130626
46552CB00006B/2348